ROYAL GUARD OF DRAGA

A DRAGA COURT PREQUEL NOVELLA

EMMA DEAN

ROYAL GUARD OF DRAGA
A DRAGA COURT PREQUEL NOVELLA

All rights reserved. No part of this book may be used or reproduced in any manner whatsoever without permission, except in the case of brief quotations embodied in critical articles and reviews.

Copyright © 2017, 2018, 2019, 2020,2021, 2022 by Emma Dean

This is a work of fiction. All of the characters, locations, organizations, and events portrayed in this novel are either products of the imagination or are used fictitiously. Any resemblance to actual events or locales or persons, living or dead, is entirely coincidental.

*For my author sister Nikki Dean,
who pushed me to do something different.*

Without you this series wouldn't exist.

AUTHOR'S NOTE

This series is now complete.

Join my reader's group Emma's Enclave to get updates or join my newsletter at emmadeanromance.com

ROYAL GUARD OF DRAGA

1

ADELINA

Pedranus Seat
Planet Pedranus

"Princess," her royal guard murmured as his arm rose to escort her down the steps of the elegant starship. His deep, warm voice washed pleasantly over her and she placed her left hand over his right fist. He walked on her left and slightly behind. Alpha deferred to her higher rank despite his more dominant genetic makeup.

As they walked carefully over the slick stones – wet from the never-ending rain – she caught his dark orange blossom scent on the air. Alpha's dominance tantalized her.

He grinned when he caught her looking at him. Adelina blushed. She tucked a piece of her blacker-than-night hair behind her ear to try and disguise her reaction.

The smell of the rich soil on the planet Pedranus barely covered the fragrance of orange blossom. Adelina breathed it in with pleasure. The gray skies and the sweet rain a stark contrast to her home planet, Draga Terra. Alpha whipped out an umbrella, activating it and holding it aloft before they walked out from under the cover of the port wing. Adelina's spidersilk gown rustled ever so slightly in the chilly wind and she shivered imperceptibly.

"Shall I get your coat, Princess?" Alpha asked.

Of course he had noticed. Adelina gave him a sidelong glance. Her gaze caught on her guard's square jaw and full lips. They'd been childhood friends, but Alpha had grown into a delicious example of a male. "Thank you Alpha, but no. I will be fine until we reach the Pedranus Seat." It wasn't a lie, but Adelina also didn't want to bring unnecessary attention to herself.

As a true submissive she was ranked below every single one of her five siblings. There wasn't a Dragan born as submissive as she for as far back as the records went – back to the time of the Ancient Humans.

Before the genetic alterations scientists had added to the human genetics for survival, there had been no such thing as dominance and submission in the same way she knew it to be. Adelina couldn't imagine not knowing her place in society, or where she stood with those around her.

How one was born was reflected in their personal, natural scent. It broadcasted their abilities to everyone around them and created a safe environment where those who were dominant protected those who served. She always knew who to defer to and how to act thanks to protocol. As a royal she should have been more dominant. The royal genes were programed centuries before to always present as dominant as a way to protect the people.

Never before had a Draga royal smelled of jasmine – the sweetest of them all.

Adelina looked through her lashes at the welcome prepared for her family. The countess stood out from the rest of her household. The old male directly behind her must be the infamous Steward of Pedranus. The servants lined up and smiled at the royal family as they approached.

As dictated by protocol the king and queen preceded them, followed by Raena, Giselle, and then Adelina the third-born. Her father escorted her mother as Alpha did her, but as his rank was higher he walked on her right.

Even her mother, who was not born a royal, was still more dominant than Adelina, if not by much. Her mother always smelled of lilacs which could darken or sweeten depending on her mood. Adelina did not mind being the most submissive. And as the third-born princess of Draga she would never rule. The Draga System was a peaceful and prosperous kingdom of nine planets ruled by eight noble families, but Raena would one day rule them all, not her.

Her father and mother stopped in front of Countess

Joslynn and the young female smiled, dropping into the proper curtsey. The servants followed her example, bowing and curtseying as per their station. Adelina watched the countess and the level of her dip with a sharp eye despite keeping her head down.

Joslynn rose from her curtsey and her father respectfully gave the countess the traditional kiss of greeting. The king then moved on to the steward who gave him directions. Servants finally rose once the orders from the steward had been given. They descended upon the luggage in the starship like a well-oiled machine. Adelina missed nothing as she surreptitiously watched them interact with the royal guards and servants. Countess Joslynn ran a tight, respectful household.

After her mother greeted the countess she went to the king who waited for her with his arm held out. Gracefully the queen took it, staying in the submissive position. Her mother smiled at her father and Adelina envied them. Despite an arranged union they had fallen madly in love over the cycles.

Raena greeted the countess next as their parents walked towards the huge stone castle with the steward. Raena brushed her lips against Joslynn's and smiled as the female dropped her gaze. Raena was more dominant than all of them. Adelina suspected even more so than their father, but she managed it well and never abused it.

The crown princess would be the perfect queen. Raena was kind, fair, and brilliant. Adelina knew Raena was tough when she had to be, but she always commanded respect and loyalty. Rarely did she have to use the power she so easily held and their people adored her for it.

Raena walked with her escort towards the castle and Giselle greeted Joslynn next. The second-born princess was stiff when she kissed the countess as protocol stated. Giselle was the strong one. Not as dominant as Raena or even their brother Asher, but she was a fierce warrior.

The constant constraint of life as a royal grated on her very being and Adelina felt sorry for her. Giselle was strong and sure. She had studied the fighting arts since she was only a few cycles old. Adelina had always admired her discipline. But the argument regarding allowing her into the forces or not was a tired one. Her will clashed with their parents more than all of them put together.

As Giselle was escorted towards the castle, Adelina dropped Alpha's hand and stepped forward. The countess had fiery red hair and peridot eyes that held a vibrant inner fire. The princess placed her hands delicately on Joslynn's forearms. Somehow she was even shorter than Adelina, but only by a small margin. Adelina bent slightly and pressed her lips gently against the countess's. The scent of winterflowers seemed to surround her. Joslynn had soft lips, even softer than her skin. Adelina dropped her eyes once she stepped back, acknowledging the more dominant female.

The reactions were bred into her. The genes so strong she couldn't deny them. It was how the Ancients, the humans of old, wanted them to be. Part of the animalistic nature brought back in force, designed to create a wolf-like society. Adelina always wondered how terrible things must have gotten for them to create such a design.

Adelina could see Joslynn's smile through her lashes. "It is a pleasure to meet you, Princess. Please take refreshments in the solar and I will be with you shortly."

Adelina nodded and placed her hand over Alpha's once again. He winked at her and Adelina blushed once more. She subtly glanced back to watch her brother Asher grip Joslynn's arms a little too tight before he gave her the gentlest kiss she'd ever seen. Adelina frowned slightly, imperceptible to all but Alpha who eyed her warily. Her brother was a contradiction who caused nothing but conflict.

Asher was born a cycle after her and was the first male. The ancient patriarchal customs had been done away with when her father became king, or he would have been the heir to the Draga throne.

His black hair always shone with cold silver like obsidian. His Draga eyes were such a dark purple they were nearly black. She had seen a few amethysts with that color but not many. His eyes were always cool and difficult to read, even for her.

His spicy scent of the black rose always made her shiver. They were at completely opposite ends of the dominance spectrum. Adelina loved her brother, but he was intense and so much stronger than her in every way.

Behind Asher was the youngest, William. He was light where Asher was dark and made them all laugh; he could make them smile even when they were sad. William had the same black hair they all did but there was a shine to it, nearly purple in its warm darkness. His Draga eyes were a light purple like lilacs, a mirror to his scent.

Her last brother, Ian gave her a small wink and one corner of his mouth lifted slightly in a secret smile. Ian was beloved by them all, but he was only her half-brother. His father's mistress, Elara, had birthed him the same month that Giselle was born.

The dramatic claim the king had placed on Ian spread like wildfire across the galaxy. It was all the nobles would talk about for cycles. Ian was a legitimate Dragan heir, but came after William in the line of succession. There were mountains of contracts regarding the situation but they all doted on him, her mother included.

Alpha stopped at the double doors to the castle. The Pedranus servants held them open wide. Her guard bowed over her hand and gave her palm a sweet kiss that was not dictated by protocol. Adelina smiled and murmured her thanks as she clasped her hands in front of her demurely.

She could hear Alpha join the others in the royal guard around the starship. As she entered the castle the whisper of her spidersilk gown seemed to echo as she made her way through the arching stone hallway a few paces after Giselle, muted only slightly by the rain.

Her submissive nature made Adelina practically invisible and she used it to her advantage. Used to viewing the world through her lashes she swept the hall, noting the doors and the servants. She saw furiously whispered conversations as two maids argued over who would bring the queen her tea before a third came and overruled them both.

The windows to her left were tall and wide, set into arches allowing the maximum amount of light. It was still dreary compared to Draga Terra. The sun was a constant presence on her home planet and already she missed it. A few more weeks and she would bask in the Kala sun.

Through the arches of plas-glass Adelina could see the royal starship in the distance and the rolling green fields before it. The roses before the stone castle were vibrant and dark in their red. The black roses – the sacred *rosanera* only grew on the capitol no matter how many tried to raise them on their own planets.

Voices rose as she grew closer to the solar. Adelina paused before the large wooden doors to admire the carvings of the gods and goddesses. She traced the detailed and beautiful carving of Rakolto, God of Harvest and Seasons. Yes, Pedranus being so fertile would favor him.

With a wave of her hand over the small standing pad the doors swung inward. Adelina clasped her hands in front of her and kept her eyes down as far as she could while still sweeping a quick, probing look over the solar. Her father was absent and her mother already had her tea. The servants had secret passages then to arrive before her.

Raena was served as Adelina selected her chair in front of the expansive windows and she could see the guards form up for their exercise outside in the rain. She waited patiently as Giselle was served. Then her brothers slowly trickled in. They each chose a spot, separating into a group of males naturally. When Joslynn entered she smiled politely and sat near the queen.

Time seemed to drag on and Adelina wondered what had happened to their father. She glanced at Raena and she shook her head slightly as she sipped at her tea. Adelina might have missed it if she didn't know her so well. She kept herself from frowning, but worry gnawed at her. The king had been so tired and they were only halfway through their tour. Anyone could see the exhaustion on his face. Sickness was rare, but it did happen and all the signs were there.

Adelina murmured her thanks to the maid as she handed over a cup with fine precision. She sipped her own tea and enjoyed the warmth of the drink against the chill of Pedranus. She allowed her mind to wander and she looked out the window as her mother started a benign conversation.

Every two cycles the royal family took a tour of the system. They had started in the Outer Rim. The cramped spaces and limited supplies made the people seem desperate. Adelina hated how neglected she felt the people were. The ninth planet, Seprilles, had a nearly uninhabitable surface despite attempts to fully terraform.

They mined metals and asteroids, but their main export was soldiers. She knew they received shipments in exchange for being an outpost for the Draga Royal Army, but it didn't seem like they were getting there in a reasonable amount of time. Someone was shorting the people of Seprilles and Adelina had made a note to talk with Raena about it once they were home.

Alpha stripped to the waist outside with the other guards and instantly snagged Adelina's wandering attention. She watched the way he moved, how the rain dripped down the muscles of his chest. She wished he would train with a shirt. He was temptation enough with clothes on. Alpha moved through his katas like a fish through water. He was graceful, beautiful, and deadly all at once.

Her guard was her closest companion. She confided in Alpha and they'd grown up in the palace together long before he'd ever been her guard. This cycle she would come of age, and it felt as though he'd grown more distant the closer the day came.

Adelina wondered if it was because he knew he would have to take her to the House of Kismet. Not everyone could afford the training, but it made Adelina all the more valuable if she knew the bedroom arts; the *camerraleto*.

The wind ruffled his blond hair and he glanced back at the castle. His eyes were as blue as the ocean and they met her amethyst ones without hesitation. He was not the same awkward boy he used to be. His training had changed him and she liked the male he'd become. Alpha was reliable, trustworthy, and strong. He made her feel safe and no one else could perform that duty better.

Adelina took another sip of her bergamot tea and contemplated how things had changed between them over the cycles. It had started as a young girl's crush and each day it grew as they became closer.

It wasn't just Alpha's muscles, his pretty eyes, or even the way he protected her. It was their conversations each day. It was his constant presence. Occasionally there was the brief brush of skin on skin, but it was his duty to keep her safe as he always reminded her. He could not do that if she distracted him.

It pleased her she could distract him at all. The only time she could get him to relax even a little was when he was her dance partner. Adelina tapped her fingernail on the rim of her cup. She would gladly have given Alpha her virginity cycles ago, but he refused to touch her more than a friend would be allowed. It aggravated her to no end. She simply had to find the right moment to clearly state her feelings because her little hints were not working.

The queen laughed and Giselle gave Adelina a look as if to say, 'Please save me from this nonsense.' Her sister touched her hand and Adelina lifted her eyes to meet her violet ones. Giselle raised a brow. Adelina shrugged one shoulder so minutely it was invisible to all but her sister.

The two of them had plenty of practice hiding their silent conversations from their mother and grandmother. Her feelings for her guard were a closely held secret, but Giselle had known from day one.

Adelina looked around the room at her family. No one acknowledged the king's absence which she felt was strange and the steward still hadn't reappeared.

"Will you be coming to Adelina's coming-of-age party?" Raena asked the young countess, instantly bringing Adelina's attention back to the conversation.

Her sister delicately tucked her raven-black hair behind her ear and glanced at Adelina with a smile. All Draga royals were born with purple eyes, but the shades varied depending on their personality. Raena was extremely dominant and her aubergine eyes reflected that spice she had.

Joslynn smiled so wide at the crown princess, Adelina wanted to smile with her. The countess had such an infectious joy. "Of course, I am so delighted to have been invited." She grinned at Adelina and bowed her head ever-so-slightly in thanks.

Countess Joslynn was young from what Adelina remembered. She would have to check the files on her shreve later to be sure. If she was correct Joslynn was only twenty-five cycles old. The countess's parents had died when she was only a babe in a terrible accident. Their starship had been attacked by pirates near the Outer Rim on their way home from Scyria.

Pirates and mercenaries were a constant threat for any of the Pedranus family as their planet was extremely rich and fertile. There was a never-ending supply of precious gems and metals. The constant rain provided rich fruit and vegetables their kingdom couldn't do without. Pedranus was a place of true beauty. It was one of Adelina's favorite planets though the rain hid the sun during most seasons and she felt homesick without it.

Adelina smiled slightly at the countess's attention and listened as the queen started listing off the guests who would be there. Their mother smiled at Raena every time she mentioned someone who could be a possible match.

The endless talk of who Raena may marry. It seemed the subject never exhausted itself. The one small grace from the Three-faced Goddess was that Countess Joslynn was such a delight otherwise the stale conversation would bore to tears.

The queen must have heard Adelina sigh. "Adelina, be respectful," her mother snapped in Ilashyan. The language only known to females rippled through the room and Adelina straightened in her chair under the weight of all those eyes.

Her brothers stilled at the musical sounds. They did not understand the words but the tone was clear. Adelina clasped her hands delicately and set them on her lap with a small smile on her face, but she wasn't paying attention. At the moment she didn't care about current fashions, or what the best color for a royal wedding dress would be.

No, Adelina wanted to see the infamous mines with Joslynn or tour the warehouses. The warehouses of gems were on the agenda for the next day and she couldn't wait. She wondered if there was a discreet way to ask the countess about purchasing some of the precious gems for her own projects.

Colin entered the solar alone and went straight for

her brothers after bowing to the females. Adelina listened to the steward ask if they would like to head to the stables to see some of the *galinas* they had available to ride. Adelina hid her shudder. She loved the giant cats, but as a submissive she had to be extremely careful around them due to their intensely aggressive nature.

William, Asher, and Ian stood with the steward Colin. They bowed before exiting the solar and Adelina watched them go wistfully.

As soon as the males had left the tone of the conversation changed. "Joslynn, I wanted to congratulate you on the wonderful job you have done with Pedranus," the queen said in Ilashyan. "I love to see my fellow sisters succeeding. Occasionally the males still assume incorrectly we are the weaker sex, though we all know our strengths are simply different."

Joslynn laughed and it tinkled through the room. "It is no longer the way of thinking here," she admitted. "After ten cycles of my rule, females are practically worshipped for their ingenuity and silent strengths."

Queen Adele nodded. "I very much look forward to seeing you when Mala returns to the skies of Draga Terra."

The tiny countess inclined her head respectfully. "I will have to ensure all is well with this quarter-cycle's production. Without my direction it can become difficult to stay on target."

"I understand completely," her mother said with one of her little knowing smiles. "Tell me of your people's thoughts regarding the royal family here on Pedranus?"

Raena watched the fiery little countess with a predator's eyes. She never missed an opportunity to get a closer look at her subjects, a better insight to their needs and wants. She also had a nose for lies. Adelina didn't know how she did it, but she could smell one across the galaxy.

Joslynn's face grew serious and Adelina listened intently. These were the conversations she lived for. "We are loyal to the Draga Crown," she stated with near-reverence. "My people are dedicated. I have heard some talk about their concern over the Avvis family and their competition with Treon, though the distance has always favored Avvis." Joslynn glanced hesitantly at Raena and seemed to second-guess herself.

Raena gave her a nod and a small smile of encouragement. "I am sure I've heard worse," the crown princess said.

"They are concerned there is no move towards a search for a husband. There are too many eligible nobles and Raena has not favored any at court." Joslynn dared a little shrug and Adelina admired her blatant break in protocol.

Raena didn't wait for her mother's next question. "What talk has there been of the Neprijat?"

Adelina physically recoiled at the mention of the race that raped and ravaged entire planets and systems. There had been rumors and whispers from the Outer Rim that the horde was on their way to their neighboring system and ally. Adelina didn't put much stock in rumors.

The Neprijat had been a horror story she was told as

a child, a race so dreaded they were still talked about in hushed tones. They'd disappeared over six hundred cycles before. Her great-grandfather was said to have fought them back before he created the peace they still enjoyed to this very day.

The Neprijat were supposed to be a sister-race descended from the same Ancient Humans as the Kalan's, the Corinthians, and the Drakesthai. From the stories of the old ones they feasted on flesh and had teeth as sharp and numerous as sharks. Adelina couldn't help the shudder of fear as she saw Joslynn grow even paler.

"We've only heard word from the traders." Joslynn couldn't look up and meet Raena's gaze as the scent of *rosanera* grew stronger. She twisted the folds of her gown in her hands. "As you know Scyria is the steadfast ally of Pedranus and always has been. They protect the borders and the planets on the Outer Rim. They would know more than I."

Raena shook her head and leaned forward infinitesimally. It was a subtle ploy of body language and it made her words feel urgent. "We were just on Scyria two weeks ago. They know only the rumors. Supposedly they move for the Khara System, but there have been no sightings of them for the last six hundred cycles."

Joslynn nodded but her entire body trembled. "Yes Crown Princess that is what I have heard as well. I personally do not know where these rumors are coming from, but I wish they would stop."

The queen frowned at her eldest in warning and Raena

leaned back, hands languishing on the arms of her chair. Her mouth moved into a tiny smile as her eyes narrowed. It was her 'queen' look. It could be frightening, but Raena planned and strategized behind that mask. She didn't actually want to watch an execution despite the expression on her face.

There was a knock at the door and Adelina looked up to see a physician in the doorway. What could she possibly want? Adelina looked to her mother and the queen's face was white as a sheet under her naturally golden skin.

"My queen, he has taken a turn for the worse."

Adelina had never seen her mother stand so quickly. She practically ran out of the solar and Queen Adele never broke protocol. A sick feeling brewed in Adelina's gut and she shared worried looks with her sisters. She would never get away with following her mother unless Raena went first.

Her oldest sister gave them a nod and moved. Raena actually ran. Giselle and Adelina were hot on her heels. Something was wrong and it was bad enough to make their mother toss aside her decorum. They turned a corner, no thought to Joslynn and how they had abandoned her.

When Raena finally stopped deep in the castle she stood in the doorway to their parents' guest room. It was the most luxurious room the Pedranus seat had to offer and the wealth of the planet was obvious in every detail. Gems glittered from the vases, the sol-powered lamps, and the artistic border just below the ceiling. The expansive room was even fitted with the most advanced tech gold could buy, imported from Khara.

None of this caught Adelina's eye as her gaze was glued to the bed where her father lay. His skin was a sickly gray rather than his normal golden tan. His cheeks were hollow and his eyes fluttered weakly as he tried to open them. King Orion was a strong male in his prime and he was an excellent ruler. He shouldn't be laying sick in a bed at only a hundred and forty cycles old. Adelina couldn't believe her eyes. With all their advancements in medicine and science her father lay sick?

Their mother knelt on the floor next to the bed with her hands wrapped around one of their father's. Her forehead touched the back of her hand and murmurs to the Three-faced Goddess were all Adelina could make out. Their mother looked up when she heard Raena's sharp intake of breath. She beckoned the three of them forward with tears in her eyes.

Adelina felt shaky as she took a step forward, and then another.

Protocol was left at the door when Raena climbed into the bed with their father. Giselle went up next and their father finally opened his eyes to smile at them weakly. Adelina couldn't bring herself to cross the room. She needed answers. She needed to know if this was curable – whatever it was.

"What ails him?" she asked the physician.

The female wrung her hands. "We are not positive, your highness. Nothing I have given him has helped. All the king's test results have come back abnormal. We're still testing to pin down what exactly is wrong, but the cure-all didn't work."

They still had no idea what her father was sick with which was highly unusual. With all the modern gene-scrubbing, in-utero vaccinations, high-tech gene therapy, and the vast types of medicines developed for every variation of the most common and rare illnesses scattered across the Draga System and beyond, it was nearly unheard of that a disease could make one as sick as her father. Adelina could count on one hand the amount of incurable diseases scientists studied day and night.

"Do you have any speculations?" Adelina asked with trepidation, hand to her stomach as the sick feeling settled.

The poor female continued to wring her hands so hard Adelina worried she would tear her skin and shatter the bones. "Nothing good your highness, I recommended to the queen she take him back to the capitol where teams of physicians could help him."

If it was one of the incurable diseases he would need the royal physician team to keep him alive as long as possible while every scientist known to Draga would scramble to try and discover the cure, but the process was not as quick as one would hope. At most her father would have a cycle with an incurable sickness.

Tears filled Adelina's eyes and finally she crossed the room to her father and the king held out his hand for her to take. She climbed onto the bed with her sisters and laid her head on his chest.

She felt like a child again, small and scared. Her

instincts told her this was bad. Her father, who had seemed so invincible to her, only a few days ago, might die well before his time and Adelina could feel her heart cracking.

All the plans they'd had gone like so much ash.

2

ADELINA

Royal Study
Draga Royal Palace
Planet Draga Terra

The rest of the tour was cut short and cancelled. They were back on Draga Terra within the week thanks to the cutting-edge tech of the royal starships. Adelina was grateful to be home, but it was tainted with bitterness.

For the first time in too many cycles her schedule was cleared and she had no obligations, though it didn't bring her joy. She stared out at the crashing waves blindly. The warmth of the sun on her skin and the ocean breeze in her hair did nothing to brighten her spirits. The gold circlet weighed heavy on her head and pressed uncomfortably, giving her a headache. Adelina rubbed at her temple and sighed.

The team of physicians on Draga Terra hadn't had a better answer than the one on Pedranus. They were able to narrow it down to one disease, a rare form of hypomalarya that was bacterial in nature and difficult to kill per the top scientist on the subject.

The funding towards the research for the cure had been doubled as it had on the other three incurable diseases. It settled in the brain which was why it was so difficult to remove without damaging the organ irreparably, and all the gene therapy in the world couldn't help once it was already planted.

Alpha rested his hand on hers and laced their fingers together. His quiet show of support bolstered Adelina and she loosened her grip on the railing of the balcony. It was one of her favorite places in the palace. The large balcony overlooked the ocean.

The room behind her was a private parlor her family used. It was a study attached to the library on one side and her father's private office on the other. The doorway to the royal family's study was hidden and coded to their genetics only.

It was a quiet place of solitude where Adelina liked to work or simply rest and digest the day's information. She also liked being so near her father while he worked endlessly.

Her great-grandfather had given them the legacy of peace, her grandfather the legacy of prosperity, and her father had the legacy of being the first Draga royal to officially ally with the Corinthians in the Khara System.

King Orion managed the delicate balance of his

nobles' desires and the general populace's needs with finesse. Now there was talk of early retirement and soon Raena would be lost to her brothers and sisters as well, but in a completely different manner.

"Alpha, do you remember your parents?" Adelina asked.

His father had been a trusted royal guard as well, but was killed saving her grandfather from an assassination attempt. His mother died a few cycles later. They said it was from heartbreak. She had left a very young Alpha alone in the galaxy.

Her guard breathed deeply as he thought. She turned from the ocean to watch him. His blue eyes were darker than normal and his blond hair unkempt, but every bit of him screamed 'deadly threat' to everyone but Adelina and her family. The uniform hid none of the predator in him. She couldn't help noticing the way the armored fabric pulled across his broad shoulders and showcased his muscles.

"Some days I feel as though I remember them," he answered slowly. "My father is mostly just impressions."

There was a strange pang of guilt in her heart. He had no father because he had died serving her family. He had been a hero for it, but Adelina didn't like how one life was worth more than another.

It was simply how things were, and it worked well.

The people were happy and the royal family was loved. Still...Adelina knew Alpha could have the same fate one day and she despised that. The worry she had for him was like a sickness.

"Your mother?" she asked instead of bringing up the old argument. Alpha had chosen this life. That was what he always reminded her. He wanted to serve the royal family and protect them as his father had. No one had forced him.

He scratched his chin. "She was always sad, but she made sure to tell me stories about my father so I would know him. 'He was brave' was what she always told me, and ever since I could remember I wanted to be like him; to be a strong and courageous hero." The way he looked at her made her insides melt.

"You are a hero," she reassured him. "What you do is not a simple thing. You put your life on the line for me and my family." Adelina wanted to say more but she held her tongue. Telling Alpha of her feelings was something she hadn't yet had the courage to do.

Alpha shrugged and turned back to the view. "I do what is required of me, but I can't help feeling as though I could do more to keep you safe."

Adelina laughed. "You are by my side most of the day when you don't have to be. A guard within the palace isn't necessary. You know that."

He grinned at her then. "True, but your father prefers it and you know you'd be lonely without my company since I am quite entertaining." Alpha whipped off his cap. His ruffled mop of hair stuck up in all directions and then he crossed his eyes and bowed while making a flatulent noise.

Adelina covered her mouth, but she couldn't help bursting out in laughter. He used to do the same thing when they were children to get her into trouble and it worked every time. She checked the study to make sure her mother wouldn't suddenly appear to scold her. "Alpha stop that, you know how much I hate it."

He grinned up at her and then stood straight, stiff as a board. Her guard stomped around the room like a wooden doll and purposefully bumped into furniture which redirected his march. Adelina giggled; glad there was no one else in the study. It was a rare moment when she wasn't constantly being watched.

Alpha returned to her side and carefully placed his cap back on. "I am glad I can still make you laugh in such dark times," he said softly. His blue eyes were full of sorrow and regret as he studied her amethyst ones. "You know the king has been like a father to me since he took me in. I'm still shocked at the news."

She leaned into him ever so slightly. They both stared silently at the waves far below them. Adelina took a deep breath and tried to gather her courage. "Alpha you know I couldn't do any of this without you. Ever since we were young you have been there and helped me through it all. The lessons, the protocol, the punishments, and the weight of everyone's eyes; through all of it you were my rock."

Turning to face him she let her hip brush against his leg, the distance between them so small. Adelina looked up and his face was suddenly serious. Her gaze traced the line of his jaw and lips before settling on his eyes.

Alpha studied her carefully. He didn't step back or try to put more distance between them, but neither did he say a word. She took it as encouragement, placed a hand on his arm and took a half step closer until her skirts brushed against his legs and his eyes widened in surprise.

"What I'm trying to say, is..." Adelina couldn't bring herself to actually speak the words; they caught in her throat. She was so full of nerves. Her heart pounded and her stomach was in knots. She would show him instead.

Slowly Adelina leaned forward so he would know what to expect, giving him the chance to stop her if he wanted. She slid her hands up his arms and wrapped them around his neck before pressing her lips softly against his. So light, she barely felt her skin on his but she could smell his soap and his natural orange blossom scent. She felt the invisible bristles of his facial hair and it tickled.

Alpha didn't move for a second. His whole body tensed and then it was like he let go of everything that held him back. His arms went around Adelina's waist and held her close. Alpha's touch was soft and gentle – barely there – but he kissed her back with force.

She practically melted in his arms. Adelina was so relieved. She was also giddy with a bubbling excitement close to fear. Her head felt light and her whole body trembled. Where their skin pressed together practically burned. Finally she pulled back and looked into his eyes, searching for the answers she wanted, for the feelings he rarely spoke of.

His hand came up and touched her hair softly, tracing the line of her jaw and then her neck. Alpha's eyes feasted on her as his hand trailed fire across her collarbone to her shoulder. The strapless gown gave him so much bare skin to touch. Adelina shivered. She let her own hands wander over the buttons and insignia on his chest, feeling the hard muscle underneath. Adelina knew exactly what he looked like beneath the fabric and she couldn't help licking her lips at the memory of sweat dripping down muscle.

Her simulcast chirped and Adelina muttered an extremely un-princess-like curse under her breath. She pulled the device out of her dress pocket and checked to see who sent the cast. Raena wanted to know where she was. The slim piece of plas-glass glowed with the request. With a quick swipe Adelina responded and slipped the simulcast back into her dress pocket.

Alpha didn't move his fingers from her skin as he studied her like she was the finest piece of art, almost perplexed in the way his brow creased. "Princess—"

She cut him off before he could say another word. "Alpha, please, how many times do I have to ask you to call me Lina like the rest of my family does?" Her hand went to his cheek and her thumb traced his bottom lip. Adelina wanted to bite it; to taste him again.

He took her hand from his face and held it with a sad look and she could already feel the words she didn't want to hear weighing down on her. As if the gravity on Draga Terra had tripled in nanoseconds.

Adelina stepped back and turned to the study door. Her sister was on her way to fetch her and Raena might have the answers she needed. "I have to speak with my siblings. We will be in Ian's lab. Can I count on you for a walk in the gardens later?" she asked lightly, redirecting the conversation so he couldn't try and put the difference in their rank between them once again.

"Of course, Princess, I will always be here whenever you may need me." Alpha brushed a quick kiss across her cheek before slipping on the persona of terrifying palace guard.

By the time Raena walked through the study door, Adelina was ready for her and Alpha was posted in the corner near the window as usual. "Sister, will you join me?" Raena asked, glancing between the two of them. There was nothing she could outwardly see, but Raena was excellent at sniffing out secrets.

Quickly Adelina crossed the room and offered her oldest sister her arm to link with. "Thank you for escorting me," she said politely, carefully following protocol to the letter. Raena was her sister, but she was also the crown princess and much higher in rank and dominance than Adelina. "May I ask you a personal question?" she asked in Ilashyan as they walked gracefully down the stone hallway towards the servants' stairs.

Raena snuck a side-glance at her. "I wave protocol," she said eagerly. "What do you want to ask?" she responded in that musical language, keeping the topic a secret from listening ears. "Is this about your guard?"

Adelina made an irritated noise. "Is it that apparent?" she demanded.

The servants' stairs spiraled down to the sub-level of the palace where all the work behind the scenes was done. None of them paid any attention to the two princesses as they made their way by the massive kitchens and the pantries.

Ian's lab was tucked away with the rest of the scientists and doctors. Their labs stretched for kilometers underground with multiple different access points. The soil helped keep the labs cool against the ever-present sun Kala.

Raena stopped in front of a glass panel, separating the area that kept the palace running and the labs. Her DNA was scanned and then Adelina's. The panel slid open to allow them access. "Welcome Princess Raena, Princess Adelina." Even the AI's were programmed with protocol.

"It is not apparent unless you know what to look for," Raena assured Adelina. "Your cheeks are still red and flushed. It is not normal for you to appear so flustered despite how much in this galaxy makes you blush."

Adelina smiled at the scientists who looked up and bowed for them. They went right back to work the second they passed, researching cures and new genetic structures to prolong their life even further.

They reached Ian's lab tucked in the corner and their genetic scan opened the door. Adelina turned to Raena, holding her back for a nanosecond. "I wanted to ask your advice. I kissed Alpha and...I am not sure what to think."

Raena grinned. "Finally, you've only loved him since you were twelve cycles old."

Adelina barely restrained herself from rolling her eyes to hide her embarrassment. "Yes, but I cannot get him to tell me of his feelings, or accept that our difference in rank doesn't matter."

"Hey! No Ilashyan allowed!" William protested. "Get in here and leave your secrets at the door."

Raena gave their brother a wink. "Let me think on it little sister. I have never been with a guard, but I believe I can help." She swept into the room like the queen she would soon be, and then plopped on the couch as their sister and nothing more. Protocol wasn't allowed in Ian's lab either.

Giselle was already curled up in an arm chair with a cup of tea talking with Ian. His lover P'draic was nowhere to be seen. Their half-brother must have asked him to leave for this meeting.

Adelina sat next to Raena and slipped her shoes off and tucked her legs under her skirt, getting comfortable. Occasionally she wondered if their parents knew of these little meetings. Ian handed them both a steaming cup of sweetened tea with milk and then sat with William on the opposite couch.

They waited on Asher as usual. He was different from the rest of them. He was always so moody and reserved. It had given him a nickname among the courtiers and citizens, 'the dark prince.'

Adelina wished they could be closer than they were, but it could be difficult to talk to him. Their difference in dominance was almost too much for her to overcome since he never seemed to ease the weight of it like Raena did.

Finally Asher walked in with his hands in his pockets

and a scowl on his face. He hadn't said much since the news of their father's health had become official. It had hit them all hard. Asher perched on one of the desks, apart from them but attentive.

Despite all this, he had always protected Adelina, always watched out for her.

Raena was the first to speak. "Father has decided he will retire this cycle, before the third moon disappears from the sky."

"So soon?" Giselle exclaimed. "That leaves little time for preparations. Six months at most. Do we know how much time father has left?"

The topic had been too difficult for their mother to go into detail on. Few specifics had been released to the public and there had been no official announcement regarding Raena's ascension to the throne, much earlier than anticipated – nearly a hundred cycles early. She would be the youngest queen in history.

Raena nodded sadly. "Father has a cycle left if the Three-faced Goddess favors him, maybe more. He would like to enjoy a little retirement with mother while he still can. It's an enormous burden to bear, but this is what I was born for."

They were all silent as they processed her words. This would change things and quickly. Adelina thought she would have the next few decades to spend with her sisters but Raena would be so far removed from their lives Adelina wouldn't be able to share in the little moments she had looked forward to. Small things such as advice with her love life.

Raena would soon have a vested interest in who Adelina would wed and her words would be weighted differently.

Adelina wasn't only losing her father; she was losing one of her sisters as well. She couldn't help the tears and felt ashamed despite the privacy of Ian's lab. She was not supposed to cry. Emotions displayed so blatantly were frowned upon, but Adelina couldn't help herself. She loved Raena and she loved her father.

"What do you need from us sister?" Giselle asked.

Everything shifted once more. Giselle would now be the Heir of Draga. She was second-born, but as soon as Raena was crowned queen, Giselle would be crown princess until Raena had a child.

This was all happening too quickly. They were supposed to have time; time to find love, time to find a spouse, time to have their own offspring. How far would their mother push to ensure the Draga throne was safe from their cousins?

Adelina looked at each of her siblings. There were six of them in total. Their cousins should never see the throne, but tragedy struck hard and fast with no mind to mercy. Could their favor from the gods be deserting them?

Raena finished her tea and set the cup down. The tinkle of priceless china was loud in the lab. William's face was pale and wan. Change was not easy for any of them. The realization of how drastically things would alter and how quickly was apparent on all of their faces.

Even Asher looked sad. The way he studied the ground in silence broke Adelina's heart.

She scooted over on the couch. "Asher, come sit with me?" Her younger brother looked relieved and took her offer graciously. Adelina held his hand as they waited for Raena's reply.

Tears streamed down her oldest sister's cheeks and Adelina knew Raena saw the end to their closeness as well. "I would like for us to spend as much time together as a family as possible over the next six months. Father included. I know once the announcement is made public I will have to separate myself somewhat. Protocol and family don't mix well as a ruler." She wiped away her tears furiously, angry at them.

Raena was beauty incarnate, even when she cried. Her raven hair, golden brown skin, and dark aubergine eyes were the talk of the kingdom. She made everything look exquisite. "Because of this I would like to ask you now to tell me what you would like from me as queen. This is something none of us expected. You will be serving me instead of father and I know this will be difficult."

Adelina had much to say on the subject, but kept her thoughts to herself. She would serve Raena however she needed. Her hobbies would not interfere with her work as a royal. No one ever had to find out about how she actually made a business out of the art she supposedly dabbled in.

Her second hobby would serve Raena well. Ever since her lessons as a child she'd been interested in the people of her system, what they did, how they did it, and the ever intricate and complicated relationships.

Ever since she'd visited Khara Prime she'd wanted to go back, to travel the universe, and to use what she'd learned to help her people and her family.

"As you know I've been training since I could walk," Giselle began. She was always the one who took the first precarious step, brave and strong. "I'm an excellent fighter and trained for war despite our centuries of peace. I want to protect our people and keep us safe."

Adelina couldn't help thinking of the rumors and whispers surrounding the Neprijat. A sick feeling hit her stomach and she couldn't stand the idea of her sister going up against something as depraved as that.

Raena nodded. "I'll do what I can. It may have to wait until I can produce an heir. You will be too important until then." Raena grinned and tugged one of Giselle's curls. "Though you know you'll always be important."

They laughed and Ian spoke up, shocking them all into silence. "I'd like to work on a cure for hypomalarya. I'm nearly done with my training as a physician, but I'd like to extend it to the specialty of diagnosis and cures. If there is anything I can do to try and save our father, I'm going to do it."

His Draga eyes flashed but the rest of his appearance set him apart from the queen's children. Despite his sandy blond hair the same color as their beaches, he had the air of a true Draga.

The royal blood in his veins made him more

dominant than most, but he was still considered a submissive among them. He was a bit higher than Adelina, which may have been hard for anyone else in the royal family to swallow, but Adelina adored Ian and it had never bothered her.

Asher shrugged when they looked to him. He was still young and had time to figure out what he could do to help Draga. He would serve, but Raena may have to decide for him. Adelina squeezed Asher's hand and he leaned into her. She wished they could talk about these things.

William shook his head. Normally he was the one always laughing or smiling. He always had a joke to tell and could make anyone smile, even Asher. He ran his fingers through his hair and made it stand up straight.

"This is absolutely insane. I'm supposed to be deployed for a few months. Is that going to change?" he asked Raena. William had enlisted in the Draga Royal Army the second he turned eighteen cycles.

Raena shook her head. "I honestly don't know, Will. Your military career shouldn't be affected, but you may not be deployed as far away as you'd like. During the transition I'll need everyone here for support, to show solidarity to our people and give them an example to follow. We do not abandon each other during difficult and trying times."

William frowned but nodded. "I have my sights set on Attorney General, but I plan on a lifetime of work and service. I'd like to go to the Outer Rim, but it can wait." He shrugged as if it didn't matter.

It did matter. Every single one of their lives would change and the weight of their position would increase as the entire kingdom looked to them during this unprecedented change.

Each ruler was supposed to spend the first hundred cycles or so of their life training and enjoying themselves, apprenticing to the current ruler. Then they would rule for a hundred cycles at which point they would retire and hand over the Crown to the eldest born child. The remaining hundred cycles would be spent in retirement, enjoying their family, and their grandchildren.

King Orion was barely into his fifth decade as king.

Raena turned to Adelina. All their eyes landed on her and she cast her gaze to the floor out of habit. Protocol and submission was such an innate part of her nature it allowed her freedom. Her mother never had to worry about her as she did with Giselle. Adelina followed the rules perfectly and therefore was mostly invisible. Her siblings were the only ones who truly saw her, and even then only in private moments such as this.

"I will serve you however you need. My art was never a priority." Though it made her more money than she cared to admit. "As you know I've expressed interest in the guilds. This can wait. I can be whatever you need me to be, Rae."

Adelina picked at the folds of her skirt. She hoped her sister would make her an ambassador. It would give her the freedom to come and go; the freedom to see the galaxy.

Raena smiled at her. "Thank you little sister, I will

think on it. I'd love for you to consider designing something for me. We'll have so many events this cycle."

"Oh, me too!" Giselle exclaimed. "You always have the prettiest dresses and jewelry."

William rolled his eyes and got up to retrieve the pot of hot water on a portable warmer. He poured everyone more tea and then leaned against Ian's lab table. "Might as well design something for us all, Lina, these are so drab." William twirled in his uniform as though he wore skirts and planted a hand on his hip. "I mean, really."

Adelina couldn't help giggling at her brother, covering her mouth to try and hide it. Raena threw a piece of fruit at Will and they all laughed. Asher even smiled.

"Do it," Rae demanded. "Design everyone an outfit for each event, and make them match."

William narrowed his eyes at Raena. Ian sighed in exasperation and started cleaning up the tea. "Is that a command?" Will teased.

Raena sipped her tea delicately, her smile wicked and cunning. "Careful or I might."

Adelina looked back down at her skirts, enjoying the moment. She would gladly design her siblings whatever they wanted. At least she would be able to help them in some small way.

3

ADELINA

Royal Courtyard
Draga Royal Palace
Planet Draga Terra

"Take a deep breath, and let it out slowly as you move through the first position into the second," Alpha instructed.

The morning was chilly and bright. Adelina's bare feet slid across the cold stone as she moved gracefully through the positions. Alpha walked around the courtyard, studying the three princess' forms as they lifted their arms and balanced on one foot, the other knee high in preparation.

"Now a high kick and flow into third position."

Adelina followed his commands, letting every thought she had go as she let out her breath slowly and evenly. The high kick was fast and hard. Her transition was smooth as she turned and crouched in preparation. *Ai-kuda* was the perfect mix of balance and grace. It didn't require brute strength and therefore was perfect for most royals. It could keep her alive. *Ai-kuda* would give her the chance to survive if trouble occurred. She would never take advantage of that.

During her grandmother's time females of Draga were not allowed to perform 'male' activities nor have masculine interests as it was not considered attractive. Adelina would have lost her mind long ago if that were the case.

If she had been common-born she could do anything she pleased with her life as long as it put food on the table.

"Concentrate, Adelina!" Alpha snapped. It was the only time he was allowed to use their first names without titles. As their instructor he ranked higher for a brief two hours every morning. "Clear your mind and do your katas right. Your life may depend on it one day."

She pushed aside her thoughts and followed her sisters through the katas. The gear she wore was loose pants and a flowing shirt. Adelina relished the freedom of motion. Perhaps she could design a gown with hidden pants.

Her mind was wandering again and she tried not to sigh. If she didn't distract herself though all she would be thinking about was how much she wished Alpha would put a goddess-be-damned shirt on.

Adelina didn't really want him to put clothes on, but she couldn't concentrate with the sun making his very skin glow, bringing the eye to every muscle all the way down his chest to the seam of his pants and the 'V' that pointed the gaze down further, like an arrow to a prize.

She stumbled.

"Princess," he murmured, suddenly at her side. His hand went to her waist to steady her and Adelina sucked in a breath. The heat from his bare skin was delicious and she could see the sweat beading on his chest. Adelina wanted to lick it and follow the trail down...

"I'm fine," she said, ignoring her sisters' pointed looks. "Please, let's continue."

As Alpha's strong shoulders walked away from her, Adelina knew she was ready to lose her virginity, and now. She made a silent vow to the Goddess she would no longer be a virgin by the time of her coming-of-age ball when she turned twenty cycles old. Any longer and the anticipation might kill her.

Alpha led them through the rest of the routine and Adelina was thankful when the second hour was up. Usually she loved her *ai-kuda* practices, but she was so distracted this morning. She planted her hands on her hips and let out a huge sigh as she looked up to the crystal blue skies as if it held all the answers she could possibly want or need.

Raena brought her a towel and Adelina delicately wiped at the sweat dripping down her forehead and neck. She was covered in it.

"I will have time for a walk after breakfast, little sister. Would you like to join me?" Raena glanced at Alpha and gave Adelina a conspiratorial wink.

Adelina watched Alpha take a drink of water and nodded. She had to do something or she would lose her mind waiting for him to make a move.

Raena and Giselle left to the palace to get cleaned up before breakfast with the rest of their family. Adelina and Alpha were alone. She went up to him and brushed her arm against his as she reached for another glass set up on the table. Adelina took a long drink, staring at him over the rim of her cup.

Alpha smiled and set his glass down. "You seemed to have difficulty today, Princess. Is there anything I can help you with?" His question was genuine and not at all flirtatious.

Adelina tried to hide her disappointment. She smiled softly. "Yes please, the transition from fourth position to eighth has always caused problems for me. I simply don't think I am agile enough to make the jump."

His eyes trailed down her body as he thought about her words. It was a completely academic inspection. She nearly growled in frustration. This male could be so dense and she was too proper. Adelina would have to step far out of her comfort zone just to remind him of her feelings and to have him voice his.

Alpha went to the center of their practice courtyard and went through the fourth position and then gracefully leapt, twisting midair into the eighth position. He landed on his feet like a cat. She admired the way his muscles flexed and how his body moved. His jump was lower to the ground than hers. There was no wasted motion. Alpha was a work of art.

It was a part of *ai-kuda* that was more for show than practicality, but it helped her immensely when it came to bodily strength and grace. Her dance lessons were a breeze thanks to Alpha's practices.

"Come here, let me show you," he said, beckoning her forward.

This was what she had wanted, a hand's on approach.

One of his large hands went to her waist as he positioned her from behind. She tried not to press herself back against him. Once he'd moved her body into the perfect form he circled her. Adelina glanced up at him.

He bit his lower lip and studied her critically. "Perform the jump," he said, waving his hand for her to begin.

She did as he asked, but still stumbled on the landing. Something about the low twist confused her. He shook his head. "You are jumping too high. This is not a dance, it is a defense form."

Adelina laughed as she wiped sweat from her brow. "I will never use that move in my life and you know it as well as I."

Alpha playfully arched a brow and leaned over her with his arms crossed over his bare chest. "Perhaps that is so, but I want the show to be perfect." His face was suddenly so close to hers.

Adelina's breath hitched. She was about to close the distance when Alpha pulled back. "Do it again."

Was he teasing her? Perhaps he wasn't as dense as he let on.

This time when he positioned her he slipped his arm around her waist and pulled her in close. Adelina felt his entire body against hers and couldn't help herself. She pressed against him, feeling every lean muscle and all the hard lines of his body. Alpha ran his hand down her arm and positioned it, and then he trailed down her side, a hair's breadth away from her breast.

When he moved her hip slightly, his fingers holding onto the curve of the bone, she imagined what it might be like if she weren't wearing any clothes. Adelina's chest rose and fell as her breathing quickened and her limbs trembled. Despite all this she held the fourth position until Alpha was satisfied. His hands gently moved over her body, leaving a burning trail that made her stomach clench and a fire start between her legs.

"Now jump," he said; his voice low and husky.

There was absolutely no chance she would be able to manage with the way her entire body shook from his touch but she tried it anyways. The landing was even worse this time and she fell. Alpha caught her before she could hit the stone of the courtyard.

They tumbled together and she ended up on top of him. Adelina looked down into his blue eyes and they both breathed heavy in the tense silence. His arms were still around her and Adelina had never been so close to him before. Her breasts pressed into his chest and the hard line of his cock was against her stomach. Her hips shifted and Alpha's fingers tightened almost painfully on her waist.

She reached up and ran her fingers through his hair,

something she'd always wanted to do. It was silky. Almost like raw spidersilk. She leaned forward and brushed her lips against his, eyes closing as the sensation of him swallowed her whole.

One of his hands buried in her hair and he kissed her harder, his other hand pressed against her lower back. Adelina squirmed at the feeling of him against her and the ache between her legs made her lose all sense of what was proper. She wanted him so badly she couldn't control herself.

She sat up and pulled him with her, raking her fingers over his bare shoulders and he groaned into her mouth, setting her ablaze. Alpha cupped her ass with both hands and squeezed, lifting her up and repositioning her right against his cock. The taste of his lips and his arms around her was everything she'd ever wanted.

Her hands trailed down his chiseled chest to the seam of his pants and he stopped her. "Princess," he said. "I don't think this is a good idea."

His words were a slap across the face and she felt like someone had poured freezing cold water over her. Adelina pulled back instantly and yanked her hands out of his as she got to her feet. She didn't even bother to look at his face to see what he might possibly be thinking. Her cheeks were so hot with embarrassment she thought she might die.

Adelina pulled her wrapped shirt back into place and straightened her pants. "I understand." May the Goddess help her, she was such a fool.

"I don't think you do," Alpha said, taking hold of her

arm and turning her towards him. "I didn't intend for you to think I meant you." He tugged her closer until he could hold her against him, burying his face in her neck as he breathed deep. "I did not think taking you here in the courtyard for anyone to see would be appropriate," he murmured against her skin.

His words made her shiver and she held on to him almost desperately. Adelina wanted to say the rest of the galaxy be damned and that wasn't like her. That thought alone had her nodding in agreement despite her body's loud protests.

"I need to go," she told him, ripping away without warning.

Quickly she walked to the palace, nearly jogging as she made her way to her rooms. It went against everything she wanted, but two more seconds and she would have ripped off her own clothes. The sexual desire shocked her. Adelina had never had issues controlling herself before.

Finally she reached her room and slipped in. Adelina closed the door and leaned back against it, breathing hard. This must be the living fire the courtesans spoke of.

She needed a shower, preferably a cold one. Stripping out of her exercise gear she walked naked across her rooms to the private bath. With a touch of a button the water started to fill the large tub and Adelina still felt feverish, like her skin itched to be touched.

The ache between her legs made her entire body feel tight and rather painful. Adelina let down her hair and the soft strands against her skin made the tingling worse. She had to get in the water before she burst.

Was this a normal reaction, or was this part of her coming of age? It was about six months early but Adelina didn't know as much as she thought she was supposed to.

Mother was to educate them on the matter, but as the third-born her education was left to tutors and no one had seen fit to teach her what to expect when it came to her own body. The books on the subject were rather lacking.

Stepping into the warm water eased some of the sensation across her skin and Adelina slid down to let the water soothe. Something had to be wrong with her. The water against her nether lips made the ache worse as if it taunted her with how empty she was and reminded her how much she still needed to be filled. Courtesans were the ones who normally had this problem, not someone like Adelina.

The image of Alpha shirtless was stuck in her mind. The detail of his warm, honey-colored skin couldn't be erased or the way the sweat rolled down his defined muscles. And his arms, the Goddess help her; those arms would be the end of her. The way he'd surrounded her with them, held her close. The feel of him against her had been her undoing.

Adelina closed her eyes and let her hands wander. The feel of Alpha was branded in her memory. His cock had been hard for her, he'd wanted her and by the feel of him he would fill her to the breaking point. It would be a pain she would relish.

Her fingers teased a nipple and traced the sensitive skin under her breast as the other traveled lower. Her left hand trailed over her belly down to the ache between her legs she couldn't ignore.

Two fingers slid over her clit and brushed against her opening. The sensation made Adelina groan out loud as she imagined her hands were Alpha's. His were large and callused, but still gentle as they teased her, slowly rubbing in a circle. The pressure built and Adelina's hand moved faster as she massaged her own breast.

Goddess, what she would give for Alpha to be the one touching her. She should have dragged him to her rooms and taken him like she wanted.

Her back arched as the ache seemed to grow. The pleasure mounted but it wasn't enough. The water sloshed against her breasts as she moved her other hand down. She slid one finger inside and then two. Adelina felt herself stretch and the sensation was glorious. Her fingers moved furiously, one hand moving in and out and the other still teased her clit. The pressure grew and she felt as though she might explode.

She wanted Alpha to hold her as he had before, his two large hands on her ass as he moved her against him. Adelina would ride him hard. His large cock would fill her and finally she would be satisfied.

She was so close, only a little more. She pressed down harder and her entire body shuddered as the orgasm hit her. The ache intensified right before it burst, washing over her in waves of pleasure. Adelina moaned and then went limp as she rode the intensity.

Heaving a huge sigh she ducked down under the water. She felt sated, but the ache had only been briefly abated. It was still there, begging to be completely eradicated and that was something Adelina couldn't do alone.

She wanted to ask Giselle or Raena if they had any experience with what was going on with her, but the conversation would be difficult to broach. Both of them had already gone through their training at the House of Kismet, but neither of them would talk about it. Adelina wondered what could be so secretive that her sisters wouldn't tell even her.

Adelina got out of the tub, dripping water across the marble floor. Once the tub sensed her absence it began to drain on its own. She looked in the mirror that covered the entire wall and noticed how red her cheeks were and her eyes were much darker than normal. She had always wanted Alpha, but her feelings for him had never caused her problems before.

She stepped under the *nila* and waved her hand. Instantly she was dry and with another selection her hair was up and styled to perfection. Adelina crossed to her closet and selected the day's dress.

The choice was perfect. She was pleased the program she had tinkered with was so effective. Every week she uploaded her schedule and choices were made based off of the day's activities. Adelina slipped it on and stepped into comfortable, yet elegant shoes.

She took a deep breath, knowing without a doubt that Alpha would be waiting outside her door like he always was. It would take every bit of protocol to keep her from skipping breakfast and tearing his clothes off.

A touch of makeup and she was done. She squared her shoulders and reminded herself she was a princess. Adelina would hold herself to the highest standard without fail, no matter what her body and mind wanted.

4

ADELINA

Royal Dining Room
Draga Royal Palace
Planet Draga Terra

Breakfast was quieter than normal. Father was missing again and the reason why was heavy on all their minds. Their mother mentioned an announcement to occur the following day, unscheduled and public. It brought terrible nerves to Adelina's stomach and she hadn't been able to eat much. There had been hope from the physician's they could stabilize the king for a few cycles, but Adelina was no longer sure it was possible.

"May I be excused, Queen Adele?"

Her mother glanced up from the fruit bowl she wasn't eating and focused her gaze. Protocol allowed Adelina to make the request despite her mother not being finished, but it made her grandmother's predatory gaze swing over to focus on her.

Her mother nodded and went back to staring at her fruit bowl. Adelina wished she could do more to help her. She stood and the males stood with her. Adelina nodded at her brothers and sisters and left the dining room as quickly as she could.

As soon as she made it into the hall she took off running. Her entire family was in the dining room and there was no one to see her break protocol.

Adelina burst through their private garden doors and stopped when the sun hit her face. Her skirts glittered in the light and she breathed deep.

It wasn't that the royal family's private dining room was small. It took up nearly the entire length of the east wing and was wide enough for a full staff of servants to serve up to thirty family members.

No, Adelina felt everyone's sadness like it weighed her down in waters so deep she would drown in the blackness and never see the sun again.

The summer-berries were blooming and the black roses covered the garden. Adelina picked a rose and breathed the spicy scent in deep. She crossed the garden to the small stone temple in the center for the Three-faced Goddess.

Adelina knelt on the hot stone, lifting up her skirts so her bare knees rested on the ground. She placed the rose at the Goddess' feet and bowed, hands splayed on the ground until her forehead touched the rose petals.

Adelina said a silent prayer for her father and begged

the Gentle God of Death to watch over the king and to hold off only a little bit longer. She wasn't ready for her father to go.

"Lina?" Raena asked quietly from behind her.

Slowly Adelina sat up and then stared into one of the Goddess's sweet faces. If the Dragas were really favored why would the gods and goddesses take her father from her so soon? "Have you spoken to the king recently?" she asked her sister.

Raena knelt next to Adelina and offered a white rose before paying her respects. The two of them stared at the statue in silence for a moment. "I spoke to him. He is announcing his abdication tomorrow."

Adelina's stomach dropped and she knew things weren't going as well as they all had hoped. "So soon?" she asked. Raena's shoulders fell and her sister looked tired. The transition would not be easy for her. Adelina turned and gave her sister a hug. "I'm so sorry."

Raena held on tight and then took a shuddering breath. "It will be okay. Like I said earlier, I was born for this. I will be all right, really," she promised Adelina.

Raena smiled and then got to her feet. Adelina followed her as they walked through the garden. "I'd like to speak on something more positive," Raena said. "How did your conversation with Alpha end?"

There was still sadness in the air, but Adelina understood the desire for a distraction. She would do whatever her sister needed and if talking about the male she loved would help, so be it. "We didn't actually have much to say."

Raena frowned and then caught Adelina's shy smile and laughed. "Well that is certainly progress!"

Adelina shook her head. "I still don't know what I am doing." Should she ask her sister about what happened? Perhaps she had experienced something similar. "There is some hesitation from him, and I believe he is keeping an emotional distance due to the difference in our positions."

Raena linked her arm in Adelina's and they enjoyed the small garden together. It was still early. The royal garden wasn't as large as the others because it was private. No one but the royal family and their personal servants was allowed and it was a grateful escape.

"All males hesitate when it comes to feelings," Raena told her. "It has nothing to do with you specifically, I am sure. You have known him your entire life. There are definitely feelings there. It can be difficult to remind him of the chance you present though, as he is your personal guard. There is no time you spend together when neither of you are who you are. He will always be your guard, and you will always be his princess, Lina."

Raena stopped and turned to face Adelina fully. Her face was sad and she lifted a delicate shoulder in a small shrug. "It is something to consider. Ask him, before you fall in love with him completely, if he would give up his position to become a prince. He may not want this life, and it is not something you, dear Lina, can give up. Your blood will be royal no matter where you go or what you do." Raena bent down and gave her a kiss on the cheek. "You cannot escape that."

Adelina knew she was right no matter how difficult it was to hear, and she kept the small detail she was already in love with this male to herself. She would find Alpha and talk with him. He still owed her a walk across the palace grounds.

"Father will announce the events occurring over the next cycle to us first," Raena told her as they turned back to the palace. "He wants to prepare us as well as he can before the public announcement. Did you get the notice on your simulcast?"

Adelina pulled out the small device from her pocket and checked through the important messages. It was right there on the top. Somehow she'd missed the cast. "So early?" she asked her sister. They were supposed to meet in the family study in only a few minutes. If it weren't for Raena, Adelina would have missed the meeting and most likely would have been punished for her break in protocol.

Raena gave her a look. "I may still be your sister and not yet your queen, but make sure you always have the simulcast on. I do not wish punishment on any of you, but you know the law. Even love is not a valid distraction."

The intricate glass doors opened for them as soon as they sensed their presence. The gold held the pieces together and the fragments reflected Kala like a massive diamond, fracturing and making the ground glitter in the light. As soon as they crossed the threshold the weight of protocol fell on Adelina's shoulders and she was once again the subordinate. Her eyes went to the floor and her hands clasped in front of her.

Raena's shoulders went back and her chin up. The distance between first and third-born was blatant in that moment as they took on the mantle of their roles. Adelina followed a step behind her sister and to the left as they walked through the marble halls. The outside wall was mostly lattice-covered windows and the plas-glass was down to allow for a breeze since the days could get very warm.

A few courtiers were up and walking the halls. Raena nodded when they passed and Adelina knew they would soon stop in the hall to bow as her new position would require. Raena breezed into the study. Adelina couldn't be more opposite. Quietly she kept to the wall and made her way around the room until she was near her father in his favorite chair.

It had been days and all she wanted was to be close to him. She gave him a kiss and then sat as near as she could manage with her mother and sisters in the room claiming priority. Adelina studied her father from under her eyelashes. He looked exhausted, but a bit better than he had been on Pedranus. She tried to take heart from that.

Giselle was the last to arrive and they all sat quietly, waiting for their father to tell them his news. Their mother held their father's hand with grace and poise, no tears to be seen.

King Orion cleared his throat and looked at each of his children. "As you know the prognosis is dire, and a cycle or more is a generous assumption. This is unexpected, but I am sure Raena will handle it with all the dignity and grace we have come to know and respect." He coughed and the wracking sound in his chest made Adelina wince in sympathy. "Tomorrow I will announce that after Adelina's coming-of-age ball Raena will ascend to the throne."

All eyes turned to her. The coming-of-age parties were always an enormous event for each child and Raena's coronation would detract from it. It would split the attention and purpose of the nobles' visit. While this could be problematic if Adelina were looking for a spouse she didn't mind really.

"The coronation will take place after Adelina's celebration, and the transfer of power will be immediate. There will be more duties passed on to Raena before then to ease the transition. I will need each and every one of you to assist her and do your part to help."

Their father sighed and rested an elbow on the arm of his chair and placed his chin in his hand with a rueful smile. "This wasn't supposed to happen for another fifty cycles at least. I apologize for the inconvenience."

Adelina didn't know what to say, or if she should even speak at all. Her father's hand found hers and he squeezed weakly. She looked up and squeezed back. "I don't mind," she whispered, knowing the small concession would ease his guilt.

"I know darling. I'm afraid we don't have the time to space it all out appropriately."

Giselle had never settled down after her coming-of-age ball, but Adelina doubted she ever would unless ordered to. With Raena as queen everything would be different and freedoms reduced before their time. Adelina needed a night to sneak out, a night she could spend free of her responsibilities.

Raena hadn't married after her coming-of-age as having options open made the most logical sense when it came to the Heir of Draga. Raena and their father had decided the bargaining chip of future king consort was more valuable than an heir.

That decision seemed foolish in hindsight, but only because Adelina knew how much Giselle would hate being the crown princess. She already felt her freedoms were hindered and that would only worsen.

Their father coughed again and their mother fussed. He shooed her back and set his jaw. The king would finish this family meeting no matter what. "This goes against tradition, but I need all of you to consider your options for marriage. In the next ten cycles you all need to be wed and producing heirs. If I am susceptible to this disease, then you all may be."

Their father wasn't contagious, but the disease could have targeted a weakness in his genes. The doctors were supposedly working night and day to find out any answers they could.

This news was no surprise to Adelina. She had assumed this would be part of 'everything they could do to help.'

Giselle though made a face and the queen hissed at her. Adelina hid her wince. If her sister wasn't careful she would end up punished again. It was almost as though she enjoyed the pain with how much she broke protocol right in front of their mother and grandmother.

Without warning King Orion stood and left the study, almost as though he couldn't stand the grief that permeated the air, thick and cloying. Adelina's eyes were dry. She would never shame her father so. He was strong and brave and would fight this sickness as he fought for his people every day of his life.

Queen Adele followed him out. Adelina and her siblings were the only ones left once again. "There really is no cure, nothing they can do?" Adelina whispered. Her eyes stayed locked on the ground, but she knew they all wondered the same.

The only one who would have answers would be Ian. Their fair brother shook his head. "I've been spending every night in my lab, studying the archives, journals, and articles we have on the subject. There is nothing, not even a trial or experimental option. The strain is resistant and there are too few cases to adequately get the answers we need." Ian looked hopeless, the bags under his eyes testament to his research.

Adelina couldn't stand it anymore. She shot to her feet. "May I be excused, Crown Princess?"

Raena nodded though she looked concerned. Adelina left the study as quickly as she could without running. She flew past Alpha standing guard at the door, waiting for her as usual. She heard him shout after her, but for once she ignored him.

She needed to get outside; she needed to be as far

away from her life as possible. She couldn't leave the palace, but she could lose herself in the grounds.

They stretched over most of Draga Terra. The forests and fields a shimmering green. Adelina considered fetching her mount for a ride, but speaking with the hostler and dealing with their constant hovering would only annoy her. Instead she walked through the rose gardens where ladies laughed and talked without a care in the world, ignorant to the life-changing news.

The forest was too far on foot, but if she walked through the maze she could lose even Alpha. Adelina's skirts flew behind her as she picked up the pace and ran. Tears streamed down her face and she didn't want anyone to see them, not even the male she loved.

Her father was dying and there was nothing she, nor anyone else, could do about it. Leaves brushed against her bare arms as she turned into the hedge maze, a project her father had loved. Adelina had even helped him sketch out the design so she knew it as well as she did the palace itself.

She turned and turned until she was near the center and finally she slowed down. Sweat dripped down her back in the heat. She breathed heavily as she made her way toward the bench that was centered perfectly in the maze.

With no one around she lay on the soft grass and looked up into the sky. Both moons hung heavy over Draga Terra. The third was still hidden and wouldn't be seen until her celebration of birth.

Adelina held up one hand palm facing out so the

smaller moon looked as though it rested between her thumb and fingers. It was something the king used to do with her when she was small. He had told her the stories of the gods and goddesses and how she could use their stars to find her place in the galaxy as the Ancients had.

Tears slipped down the side of her face and into her hair.

Someone lay next to her on the grass and said nothing. Adelina knew without looking it was Alpha. Briefly she wondered if he'd set up a tracking program on her simulcast, but it didn't matter if he had. Her safety was his job, nothing more and nothing less.

He was not required to care about her feelings, or have feelings for her at all. "Alpha, will you tell me why you chose to be my guard and not Giselle's or Asher's?" She had given the final approval after his interview, but he could have applied to anyone in the royal family.

Alpha was silent for a few seconds and then his voice rumbled over her, quiet in the serenity of the maze. "Aside from the bit about Asher being a prick, I know you, Adelina, better than I know myself. We spent cycles together playing and attending lessons. You've been my best friend since as early as I can remember."

Before she could reply he rolled on top of her and his bright blue eyes studied her intently. He brushed the tears from her face. "You are the kindest, most gentle person I've ever known and the way you treat your people...Adelina you would have been the most wonderful queen if you'd been first-born."

She shook her head even though his words made her

feel warm and loved. "You know that is not true. I would have hated it and constantly questioned every decision." She laughed through the tears at the idea. Alpha always knew what to say to make her feel better.

Alpha's smile was soft as he traced her face. "Do you remember when Giselle went through her rebellious phase and it seemed as though she were punished nearly every day? You took the blame for her once. She'd been caned the day before and another would have left her indisposed for at least a week. You took her punishment and never once cried. I promise you I would not have been as strong."

Without waiting for a response, Alpha leaned down and kissed her lips gently, tasting as his hand held her neck like she were a fragile piece of glass. He smelled like the sun and the clean scent of his soap. Adelina's hands buried in his silky soft hair and she sighed into him.

Alpha gave her strength and courage when she felt she had none. He held her up when she couldn't stand on her own.

What would she do without him?

The thought relit the fire she'd barely quenched earlier. Adelina was slightly horrified. It wasn't the time to be thinking about things like taking the male who covered her body with his, of finally losing her virginity. She felt guilty. How could she be so selfish with all that was going on?

But this was exactly what she needed right now; a distraction. Adelina needed a reminder that not everything was dire and miserable. There were still good things she could be happy about. There were people in her life who reminded her life was worth living no matter how awful it got. Alpha was someone she loved. He was someone she knew would be there for her no matter what.

The heavy weight of his body against hers was comforting. Adelina knew he was hers in the same way she knew he would protect her with his life. The last fifteen cycles they had been nearly inseparable until his guard training. Then he had come back fit and strong. She ran her hands over those muscles she couldn't stop thinking about.

That first moment she saw him after his training she'd nearly lost her mind. Alpha looked like a completely different person and his new strength only made her want him more.

Now his body was against her and she could feel the length of him through her thin skirts. Adelina wanted nothing more than to rip off the uniform and have her way with him under the sun and out in the open.

She knew this was unusual from someone as inexperienced as she, but she didn't care.

Adelina pulled his shirt out of his pants so she could grip his bare skin. He was warm to the touch, nearly feverish. The way his mouth devoured her made her dig her nails into his back. Alpha's tongue danced with hers and she couldn't help the small moan as he pressed into her.

The hard length of his cock rubbed against her clit

and the electric shock that ran through her nearly made her lose control.

Alpha growled against her mouth and lifted her up with him until she sat on his lap. He gripped her waist so hard Adelina knew she would bruise, but he didn't let his hands roam. They stayed right where they were. She made a small sound of protest and rocked against him. His cock strained against his pants and pressed into her. The ache between her legs was nearly unbearable.

"Alpha," she whispered his name like a prayer and his fingers spasmed. Adelina pressed her palms flat against his chest and rolled her hips again, slow and tantalizing. She wanted to do to him what he did to her and plenty more. "Do you love me?" she asked. It was something she needed to hear, something she'd always wanted to know. Adelina wanted to hear the words her heart already knew the truth of.

"Lina, I've loved you since the day I met you," he murmured, rubbing his nose along her neck. "The day you shared everything you had with a poor boy with no parents."

His fingers found the clasp of her dress and slowly undid the tiny piece of metal holding her dress together. The spidersilk dropped and exposed her breasts to the warm air. Her nipples hardened and Adelina gasped knowing anyone could see them if they made it this far into the maze.

She threw her head back as Alpha trailed his lips down her throat and over her collarbone to the tender flesh of her breasts. He brushed his lips against one nipple and then the next, delicate and soft.

Adelina dug her sharp nails into his shoulders. She wanted him to suck on them and then bite her. She wanted so much more than his soft touch. "Please, Alpha," she whispered, careful to keep her voice low despite how badly she wanted to growl at him for being so gentle. His name on her lips undid him.

Suddenly he was ravenous, starving to death and she the meal. His tongue laved her nipple and then he sucked hard. The sensation sent a shock to her clit and she gasped. Adelina couldn't help squirming. There was so little fabric between them and all it would take was undoing a little button.

Alpha's hand reached under her skirts to travel up her thigh and settle at the sensitive, bare skin between her hip and her leg. He was so close to where she needed him to be. Adelina shifted against him, hoping to coax him into taking them both further.

"Adelina!"

Instantly she froze. Adelina's eyes shot open and she met Alpha's panicked gaze. Had that been her mother?

"Goddess bless – Adelina! Come out of that damned maze!" Holy gods it *was* her mother.

Adelina scrambled off of Alpha and pulled her dress up. She turned so he could do the clasp and then she turned back to inspect him. His hair was wild and his uniform disheveled. The tight fabric made his arousal obvious and she couldn't help her grin. "I'll go and redirect her," she told him, kissing his cheek.

Her mother practically screeched she was so annoyed. "Adelina!"

She tried not to laugh as she responded. "Coming Queen Adele!" Adelina turned to run after her mother who was probably lost among the hedges.

Alpha grabbed her before she could leave and kissed her hard. His tongue slipped into her mouth and he held her face gently. When he let her go she felt dazed. The sound of approaching footsteps reminded her of their close call.

She ran off before her mother could find Alpha in his current state and hoped she didn't look too wild. Her hand went to her hair, but it seemed in place. Adelina slowed down when she saw the glitter of her mother's crown among the green leaves and walked to her side.

"Yes, mother?" she asked, hands clasped in front of her and eyes downcast; once again the perfect, subordinate princess.

5

ADELINA

Jeweler's Guild
Stella di Draga
Planet Draga Terra

It was nearly midnight and the sun was finally setting. Draga Terra was close to the center of the system and it made their days long and their nights short. Adelina pulled up the hood of her cloak and made her way through the tunnels below the palace.

The tunnels were old sewer and water systems no longer used since advanced tech had been put in to keep the water clean and recycled. The sewage was diverted and used for energy; nothing ever went to waste.

Her tight pants stretched as she placed a hand and leaped over a set of bars. Her knee-high boots cushioned her feet when she landed. The way out of the palace and into the outer rings of the city was familiar. Adelina didn't even have to think about it anymore.

Normally she came out with Giselle, but her sister was preoccupied with their mother's cajoling. The queen pushed too hard for her to find a husband and marry. Adelina half expected her to marry a female instead simply to infuriate the queen. But an unknown father was looked down upon; the only reason Giselle was expected to wed a male.

Goddess help whoever she chose.

Adelina placed a gloved hand against the stone wall and took a left. Only a few more city blocks and she would be close to the taverns. Her destination was the biggest tavern of them all; owned by the prince of thieves who had always been kind to her.

Her boots splashed through puddles and she knew there would be more rain once the sun had fully set. The temperature had already begun to drop. The few hours there was no sun were freezing in comparison to the day.

The jewels in her pouch clinked slightly. Adelina had a delivery to make to the guild before she could enjoy herself. The citizens never recognized her. She was always shocked what a bit of makeup, a set of colored lenses, and a different hair color could accomplish. Pants did wonders as well. She didn't mind her gowns, but there was so much freedom in being nobody anyone would recognize.

Finally she reached the markings she and Giselle had made cycles ago indicating the end of the first-circle and the beginning of the second-circle of the city. The luminescent paint the only light deep underground. Adelina grabbed the rungs and hoisted herself up the ladder and waited when she reached the top, listening carefully. No hov-carriages seemed to be in the area and footsteps were far off.

Lifting the cover she slid out of the old sewage tunnels and replaced it before anyone witnessed what she was up to. Nearly all of the covers across the capitol had been welded shut decades before when the entire system had been overhauled. Adelina and Giselle had fixed that from the inside.

All tunnels led to the palace, the epicenter of the capitol. She could go anywhere she pleased with no one the wiser.

Adelina made her way through the streets of the second-circle. The second-circle was mostly businesses and markets. It was where the well-off and the poor easily mingled. Some streets were nicer than others and the quality of the products varied from neighborhood to neighborhood, but it was clear from the name of each business and its symbol what was sold inside.

She passed Giselle's favorite bakery and went down a darker alley. The Jewelers' Guild was tucked in the middle of a good and bad neighborhood in the second-circle. It was unusual for such a profitable guild, but Adelina understood the placement.

The guild broke the sky with jeweled towers and stained glass. It stood out among the other businesses like a gleaming gem, allowing anyone with skill to apply.

The few people on the streets ignored her, heading

for the taverns and bars they preferred at this time. The hov-tram passed overhead, bathing her in bright light before plummeting her back into darkness. Adelina kept to the sides of the streets, it was safer that way.

There was a large open space before the guild and chances of someone seeing her were high. Adelina checked to make sure her hood was in place and then rolled her shoulders back. She had to look confident to avoid any unwanted confrontation. Adelina strode forward and her cloak furled behind her.

She had to slip off her glove to place her hand on the door to the guild. It recognized her prints and opened just wide enough for Adelina to slip through. It was a pretty program she had created. Adelina checked the ring and then slipped her glove back on before making her way through the dimly lit guild. Most of the masters would be at home and asleep. Any apprentices still working would be at their tables and would pay her no mind.

There was one person in the entire guild who knew her identity. The ring she'd made was embedded with a program which disguised her prints. Adelina had written an entirely new identity to work under. The same went for the lenses over her eyes to change the color. Draga amethyst would have given her away instantly. If her family ever approved of her work she would transfer the details to her real identity. That day didn't seem likely though.

Adelina silently made her way up the spiral staircase and down a hallway to the main offices. She knocked on the guild master's door and waited patiently. She heard shuffling and grumbling before a slice of the door became see-through and his eyes found hers. They widened in surprise when he recognized her disguise and the door opened an instant later.

"Lina, I didn't expect to see you for a long while based on the information I received from the palace," Calix muttered, standing aside to let her in.

His work covered one table and then the main desk held nothing more than a few shreves. The guild master's passion was still working with gems when he could.

Adelina bowed low to her master and once he acknowledged her she threw off all pretenses. He hated protocol more than she did.

"You look tired old man," she said before walking to a plush couch he had along one wall. Adelina flopped into it and stroked the velvet. "Working late again I see." The alcohol in the glass on his worktable looked strange among the glittering pieces she could see from across the room.

"What are you doing here?" he asked, settling in his chair at his worktable. The guild master was in his third century and it showed. The lines of his face, and the papery thin skin covering his bones made her think he would break apart if he were ever to fall.

Calix was known across their system for his exquisite work. He'd been commissioned for the last three coronations as well as every royal wedding and event.

When Adelina had come to him five cycles ago begging to secretly apprentice, he'd refused of course. He was a mean, crotchety old male who hated everything but his gems. Somehow she'd won him over after bringing him her work on her second attempt.

He'd kept her secret, surprisingly enough, and never bothered to blackmail her with it. Said it was too tiring the one time she'd asked.

"I had commissions, Master Calix. It would be difficult to explain why I was late on the delivery." Adelina untied the pouch from her belt and selected the items she'd been working on; two necklaces and a pair of matching earrings.

Her favorite jobs though were the engagement rings. She would imagine the love and dedication the couple had, how the person who commissioned her would detail their desires so completely. Every single ring she made held the love of the commissioner. Adelina adored that and knew she was a terrible romantic.

"I keep getting asked who my apprentice is, 'who is this Lina.' You're sure you couldn't meet with them in this?" Calix gestured at her disguise before tapping his temple.

The guild master had implanted a high tech magnifying device the moment he could afford one. Adelina was jealous. She could never get away with such an implant. It was too 'unnatural' for a princess. Calix inspected her work and muttered under his breath something that sounded like begrudging praise.

He shook his head and carefully placed the pieces in velvet cases for the customers. Then the guild master counted out her gold and handed it to her. Adelina slipped it in her pouch and carefully tied it back on her belt.

"How you come up with these designs...you have very little training yet your settings are perfect. How do you manage it?" Calix asked with a strange, one eyed glare. His other pupil was too dilated to really focus on her. He grumbled again and shook his head, tapping off the device.

Adelina shrugged, self-conscious under his admiration. "I read everything I can find and then work in my spare time. I have been doing this for many cycles now. The perfection is debatable, but if I've managed it, it is only due to your tutelage." She stood and kissed him on the cheek. He waved her away in annoyance, but a small corner of his mouth turned up in a nearly invisible smile. "Would you mind blocking out my schedule for these dates?" Adelina tapped her simulcast to the shreve on his desk with her schedule.

The weeks before her ball and all the way through her sister's coronation was blacked out with weeks to spare. There would probably be a wedding as well and if she needed to update it again it would give her an excuse to escape the palace during the madness. "There is sensitive information on that file, so please keep it private as always?" Adelina requested.

"Of course, now leave this place before someone sees you. I will send your next lesson by vid, encrypted with your little program." He shooed her out of his office and went back to his worktable.

Adelina left with a smile. She'd needed this, this

stolen freedom to be who she wished to be. With a bounce in her step she made her way down the spiral staircase and back out into the night. She stepped down into the street and heard the guild door close behind her.

It was true night. There was no sun in the sky and the two moons loomed heavy over the capitol. They were partially obscured by the clouds and with little warning except a crack of lightning, rain fell from the sky in sheets.

Adelina held out her arms and breathed in the sweet scent of night-blooming violets that only opened when the night's rain fell on their petals. Adelina loved Draga Terra with her entire being. Everything about her planet was beautiful and exquisite in its own way, especially the people. She turned and made her way through the street towards the thieves' court. She had a delivery for the prince as well.

Someone snatched her arm and yanked her into a dark doorway.

Adelina didn't even think. She reacted just as Alpha had taught her. Her hand was quick as lighting as she struck up and hard. Instantly her attacker released her and coughed, holding his throat where she'd hit him. Adelina ran down the street as fast as she could until she heard a familiar voice call her name.

She paused in the downpour and turned slowly. "Alpha?" she asked carefully. If it wasn't him she had other problems.

Her guard stumbled out of the doorway, wheezing with his hand to his neck.

"Alpha!" she exclaimed, running up to him. "I am so sorry; you shouldn't have grabbed me as you did!" Truly he should have known better, after all he was the one who taught her to take care of herself against a potential kidnapper.

Finally he regained his voice. "Good work," Alpha croaked. He massaged his neck and cleared his throat. "Now explain to me what in the seven hells you are doing out here on your own?"

Adelina arched an eyebrow at him and lifted her hood back over her hair to hide her face in the shadows. She was free of the palace and her title for one night, protocol no longer required until morning. "What does it look like I'm doing?" she asked, turning back to her original path.

He grabbed her arm again and whipped her around. Adelina pushed him off and her hand came up, ready. "You may be my guard, but I am not your princess at the moment," she warned. "Do not manhandle me."

Alpha raised his hands up in surrender and took a step back, eyeing her warily. "All right, I apologize. You scared the life out of me, Lina. I went to check on you and you weren't in your rooms."

She shrugged and turned back. He would follow or not – it was up to him, but she wasn't going back to the palace until she was ready. There were only so many hours of darkness. Adelina picked up her pace.

The larger, blue moon bathed her and the city in its light. As they grew closer to the tavern the sound of laughter and shouts grew. Adelina smiled. It had been too long since she'd last seen the prince and his court.

"Lina, please explain to me what's going on." Alpha was annoyed and miffed that she simply ignored him.

Adelina sighed and glanced sideways at him. "You've only been my official guard for a few weeks now. You are the first to notice my disappearance. Perhaps hiring someone so close to me was a mistake," she joked, making sure to smile at him so Alpha knew she didn't mean it. It was something that hadn't occurred to her though it should have.

Adelina had been sneaking out for cycles now and no one was the wiser. She'd figured out how to disable the alarms to her doors and windows once the security system had been activated for the night. It wasn't difficult to do once she'd spent an entire cycle learning how to program and work with different tech devices.

It had been a secret project of hers ever since she'd learned the palace was essentially her prison until she came of age. Twenty long cycles before she could go out in the capitol with only a guard or two. Until then it was a full regiment. The first twenty cycles of a royal's life were the most fraught with danger. Children were impressionable and easy to manipulate.

"How long have you been sneaking out?" he demanded, his voice pitched a bit higher than normal.

Adelina reached the row of taverns that separated the second-circle from the third-circle and stayed close to the buildings. She didn't want to tangle with anyone coming out of one of the taverns inebriated and with their common sense lacking. She counted as they walked. Hov-carriages were few and far between so late. Taxis were all that roamed the streets.

"About four or five cycles," Adelina finally replied. Her waterproof cloak shed the rain without soaking her clothes.

Alpha nearly stumbled. He regained his senses quickly and caught back up to her, eyes darting every which way. His mind was in overdrive, threats could be in every corner with her so exposed. It was clear across his face.

Finally she stopped him. The largest tavern in the ring was across the street, the *Ladrole*. He couldn't act like this once they entered otherwise there would be problems with the thieves' court Adelina couldn't afford.

"You need to relax," she told him. "Act as my friend and comrade or you cannot come in with me. You will have to be on your own."

Alpha glared at her. "You don't mean to go in there," he said, jerking his chin at the prince of thieves' tavern and place of business.

She cocked her head at him and crossed her arms over her chest. "That's exactly what I mean to do. Varan and I have been friends for a few cycles now, and we also do business together."

Alpha's eyes widened. His jaw dropped and he stared at her as though he'd never seen her before in his life. A part of her felt a thrill of excitement at the new respect and interest she found in his gaze. "How could I have missed this?" he asked. "We've been best friends our entire lives and you never told me." He looked rather put out.

"The only one who knows is Giselle. I couldn't tell anyone, especially not you. You wanted to be a guard since you could speak, Alpha. Why would I have told you when you would have notified everyone?" They were best friends, but he worried overmuch and it was difficult for him to simply relax.

Alpha's brow furrowed in annoyance. "Fine, I'll leave you be. We will go in as friends, but only so it looks less suspicious when my eyes never leave you." He looked down at her and there was a heat there she hadn't seen before. Adelina caught her breath as he sparked that flame alight inside of her.

Alpha touched her face and she stepped back, knowing anyone could walk out and see them, but with her disguise...He followed her until her back hit the wall of the building and she gasped when he pressed against her. His mouth was suddenly on hers and his hands gripped her roughly. Alpha's kiss was passionate and hungry. His tongue slipped into her mouth and he left her breathless.

He pulled away before she could react, before Adelina could rip the fabric from his body and score her nails across his skin. She wanted to bite his lip hard enough to bleed.

She wanted *more*.

Alpha's mouth against her ear tickled. "You never cease to amaze me." He stepped away and gave her a grin, indicating she should lead the way into the thieves' court.

Adelina took a second to catch her breath, staring at him through half-lidded eyes. "You will pay for that," she said, pushing off the wall to cross the street.

His kiss had set every nerve ending on fire and every millimeter of her skin tingled and begged for more. The ache between her legs was back and it demanded fulfillment. Alpha had no idea what he'd started. Adelina stalked to the main gate, irritable and flushed. She shook out her hands and walked through the archway into the main courtyard.

The tavern was enormous. It took up nearly an entire city block. The bottom floor was the bar and tavern. The second floor had rooms for rent, and the third floor was where Varan had his personal office and various other business offices. Adelina never asked for too many details. She was still a princess after all and could only overlook so much.

The guard nodded to her from his post in the guardhouse and she saluted him. Alpha watched everything with a wary eye, but said nothing. The shock and surprise on his face was obvious though.

When Adelina entered the tavern the loud voices hushed for a second and the pitter patter of her heart increased as she wondered, as she did every time she went out, if this was when someone would recognize her through the disguise.

The patrons went back to their alcohol, food, and conversations. They ignored her and Alpha as she crossed the room to the back corner. It had the largest table in the place and a handsome male leaned back in his chair against the wall, grinning at her the whole way across the room.

Adelina smiled in return. His playful grin was difficult to refuse. Varan's emerald eyes glinted at her and he stood when she approached. "Lina, my darling." With open arms the prince of thieves reached out for her.

Adelina gave him the kiss of greeting, a slight brush of her lips against his and then she pulled back to get a good look at him. "You look well, Prince Varan."

"Oh sweet girl, you know you can simply call me Varan, no need for strict protocol in this court." Varan gave her a wink as they sat at his table.

With a brief flick of his finger a maid was instantly at his side, setting up new glasses and pouring the sweet alcohol he favored. It was made from his own crop of winterflowers from what Adelina heard. The drink was delightful, and very, very strong.

As soon as the waitress disappeared Adelina felt more comfortable. Varan was one of the few who employed people to wait his tables and not bots. He said it was more cost effective, but Adelina knew it was because a person had more cunning than a bot and could spy for him among the many patrons who visited his tavern. The thief could give the Spider a run for their money.

"Who's your new friend?" Varan asked as he offered a plate to each of them. A large platter of various foods was placed in the center of the table and Varan selected what he wanted with his fingers.

Adelina excitedly chose her own food. Varan's chefs

were renowned, hailing from across the galaxy and she loved the variety. Alpha kept his hands in his lap and his eyes on everything that moved. He was out of his element and it showed. She would have to throw some truth in with her lie.

"He is a friend who just became a guard in the palace. I wanted to show him a good time in celebration," Adelina said with a shrug, shoveling food into her mouth with her fingers. The spices were delicious and the meat cooked to perfection. She took a sip of her drink and it paired beautifully. Clove and spicy winterflower mixed with the spice of the meat was exquisite.

Varan's eyes were sharp and he relaxed slightly at her admission. The prince had known Alpha was a guard the second he set eyes on him. "Poor taste dear girl." Slowly he sipped his drink and glared at Alpha over the rim of his glass.

She rolled her eyes. "Sweet prince, someone has to teach them to have some fun otherwise they are less tolerant of our kind." Alpha's eyes nearly bulged at her words but she ignored him. "Do you have what I asked for?" Adelina watched Varan out of the corner of her eye, focusing her gaze mainly on her food.

Alpha shifted uncomfortably and she kicked him under the table.

"Do you have what I asked for in exchange?" Varan shot back with a playful grin. There could be no mistaking the steel in his voice. The male was not the prince of thieves because he was pretty.

Adelina shoved her plate forward and threw an arm

over the back of her chair, leaning casually as she studied the prince. She took a sip of her drink and noticed how his hair shone like gold under the warm lights of his tavern.

The corner they were in cast a shadow over most of his face, but those beautiful emerald eyes had an inner fire. They held a predator's gleam as he studied her just as closely. Varan knew there was something off about her and it was his constant game to try and find out what it was.

"I do. It wasn't easy to find, but I managed." Adelina untied the pouch from her belt and set it on the table. "And you, my dear prince?" She fluttered her lashes at him playfully. Varan was a terrible flirt and she loved to play with him. It was the only practice she could get.

Varan leaned forward until their noses nearly touched. "You know I'm a male of my word," he murmured, brushing his thumb across her bottom lip. Her blood nearly boiled, but it wasn't quite the same as when Alpha touched her. Varan was handsome and oozed sexuality. Perhaps if she didn't have such strong feelings for her guard she would consider taking the prince to her bed.

The thief leaned even closer and pressed his forehead to hers like a lover. Alpha clenched his hands and went rigid. This was more than he'd bargained for, but Adelina was used to the thief and his ways. She nuzzled against Varan like a cat and felt the small, cold metal slip into her shirt, right into her brassiere. "Thank you," she breathed, making sure her lips brushed his cheek as she pulled back.

Varan didn't look like a male who had just used his seductive charm as he sat back, eyes flicking between her and Alpha. He pointed first at her and then her guard. "This isn't going to work," he stated.

His statement was so abrupt and unwanted Adelina simply stared at him. "Perhaps," she snapped. "But it's no business of yours. Do you want the gem or not?"

Varan threw his head back and laughed. "True, true my little cat. You remind me of a very tiny *galina*." He grabbed her hand and kissed the back of it. "Now let's see this gem you say you've managed to find for me despite my people's best efforts to obtain it."

Adelina reached her gloved hand into the pouch and found the hard, round stone and closed her fist over it. She flicked her eyes around the room before bringing it out. Adelina offered it to the thief, palm up. The five karat sapphire shone in the low light, dark and mysterious like the prince himself.

Varan's eyes widened and he reached for it. Adelina closed her hand before he could take it. "I trust exactly what I've asked for is on the disc?" She gave him an appraising stare. He may be a male of his word, but he could also be literal enough to skirt certain parts of his agreements.

Varan lifted a corner of his mouth in an appreciative half smile. "It wasn't easy to find." Another flick of his fingers and the waitress was back with another device.

"The rest is on this." He held the disposable shreve to her and she placed the sapphire into his other, waiting hand.

Adelina checked the shreve and found what she needed. She slid the two sides closed and tucked it into her pouch. "Thank you, Varan." With business concluded the muscles in her shoulders relaxed and Adelina downed the rest of her drink. The waitress unobtrusively filled it before she could set the glass on the table.

Varan inspected the sapphire, holding it in his palms like one would a newborn babe. "How did you manage to get your little paws on this?" he asked in wonder. "I've been looking for one for cycles."

The sapphire was special not only because of its size, but its cut. It was a sphere, faceted to reflect the light. It was darker than night without a single flaw. It was a symbol of true love and passion; therefore it also represented the goddess of love and wisdom, a holy object to be sure.

She had used her ties with the guild and her weight as a princess to acquire it, and then used her own funds to pay for it. Under normal circumstances one would not be able to find one.

"I have my ways," she said, rolling the stem of her glass between her fingers. "What do you plan to do with it?" She had a suspicion he had a lover, but couldn't be sure.

"Never you mind my sweet little cat. This pays for what you asked for and then some. I never expected you to actually be able to follow through. Some high and mighty lord is missing one of his prized possessions, I am sure." Varan gave her a wink and Alpha looked at her sharply. No, she didn't steal it, but it didn't hurt to let the prince think so. "I will be sure to send you anything on the subject as soon as I learn of it. You have any more questions or assignments, you let me know. I am in your debt."

The prince of thieves stood and bowed. Adelina quirked a smile. She loved this male for all his eccentricities. He was a friend and an excellent business partner. "I hope you don't mind if we stay and enjoy your company for a while?" she asked, raising her glass to him.

"Only if you promise to dance with me gorgeous." Varan yanked her up and music started as if on cue. He twirled her around and Adelina laughed.

She felt wild and free—and for a little while she could forget all her troubles.

6

ADELINA

Adelina's Rooms
Draga Royal Palace
Planet Draga Terra

Alpha and Adelina laughed as they ran down the street, trying to beat the early sun back to the palace. He let her pull him along to the secret tunnel. There were more hov-carriages populating the streets than before, preparing for the day bright and early. Alpha kept watch as she climbed down the ladder. He followed when the coast was clear, carefully putting the cover back in place and locking it.

They ran as quickly as they could back to the palace and Adelina was short of breath by the time they reached the cool underground sewage tunnels coming from the old wing. It went up into the retired kitchen, used before the remodel. The two of them made their way through the ghostly rooms. She pulled him up the servants' stairs to her floor and ducked down the hall.

Adelina avoided the cameras in the halls by timing their rotations perfectly, something she'd practiced over and over before her first escape. Alpha followed her lead, allowing her to keep tugging him along. The door to her rooms opened the second it recognized her prints and she yanked her guard inside with her.

"Lina, I don't think it's a good idea for me to be in here," he protested. "Someone could find out and report me."

Adelina pressed him up against her closed door and kissed him hard. The excitement of the night and his constant touch had her straining to maintain control. Her skin was tight and she felt restless. Alpha had been a surprisingly passionate dancer, something she hadn't expected from him.

The ballroom styles were the only dances he'd ever led her through before that night. The way he'd looked into Adelina's eyes had her weak-kneed and counting the minutes before it would be polite for her to leave the *Ladrole*.

She pulled back and smiled playfully. "Don't worry, I'll ensure the report never sees the light of day."

Alpha grinned. He reached down and grabbed under her thighs and pulled her up in one quick motion. Adelina's legs wrapped around his waist on instinct and she gasped in surprise. "I never suspected you to have a bit of dominance," he confessed. "I have to admit I thought you were one of the true submissives."

He walked slowly across her rooms towards her bedchamber and the massive bed in the center. Truly it was a monstrosity in size.

Twirling his hair in her fingers, she couldn't tear her gaze from him. The hunger in his eyes made her squirm. "And if I were?" she asked, voice low and husky. Adelina knew she was truly submissive – though on occasion she found the desire to be in control, to be the one who named the stakes, and it had surprised her just as much as it had Alpha.

He placed her carefully on the bed and leaned over her. "Then I would love you for exactly who you are," Alpha admitted. "But to know there is this other, secret part of you no one but I know about..." he trailed off as he stood.

Adelina couldn't believe he'd finally said it, he finally said the words out loud, and she watched Alpha take off his coat with appreciation. The shirt underneath was tight across his muscled chest. His arms were thick and strong and his veins clearly visible even in the dim light of her room. She trailed her fingers down his arms and pulled him toward her, but he resisted.

Carefully he undid the laces of her vest and helped her shrug out of it. Then her shirt was next, revealing the small lacy fabric across her breasts. Alpha bent over and brushed his lips against the hollow of her throat and then across her collarbone. He nibbled at the fabric over her nipple which made Adelina gasp and arch up to meet his warm mouth.

His attention went lower, to the bare skin of her belly

and down to the waistband of her pants. Goose-pimples ran across her skin and Adelina couldn't help the trembling. His rough hands gently undid the laces and slid the fabric over her ass and down her legs. Alpha made a rumbling noise deep in his throat as he saw she was bare under her pants and completely exposed to him.

Alpha paused for a moment and looked at her. Adelina breathed hard and waited for what he would do next. The tingling across her skin begged for release and she shifted as the hunger in his eyes made way for concern and he frowned. "Are you sure about this?" he asked.

Adelina shifted her hips. "Of course I'm sure Alpha; I wouldn't have let it get this far if I weren't."

He must be nervous about hurting her. To escort one from virgin to an experienced lover was an honor and no one could be better for Adelina than Alpha. She knew this deep in her heart and had always wanted it to be him.

He leaned over her and brushed his thumb across her lower lip and then her jaw. Alpha climbed over her, hovering as he held her face gently, memorizing every detail. "I took a vow, Princess. I have to remain objective in your safety and allow you the freedom to make a smart match. Your hand in marriage could prevent war one day."

She wrapped her arms around his neck. Alpha's broad shoulders seemed to encase her, cutting off the chill from the ocean air and making her feel safe and warm. Despite her inexperience, Adelina felt sure this was the right thing to do.

If she never acted on her feelings and desires she would always wonder if she'd missed out on the kind of love she had only read stories about. The kind of love wars were fought over – love that made peace possible if only to preserve the feeling a little longer.

"You are the only one I want," she told him. Adelina's amethyst eyes looked deep into his blue ones and she made sure he could see the truth of her words. "Who I love is the one freedom I have as princess."

Adelina pulled his head down and parted her lips slightly, allowing him to make the next move. He hesitated and then took her mouth; he possessed her with his tongue and the molten heat of his body. Alpha's hands tightened on her hips and he held her as though he'd waited his whole life to kiss her.

"Alpha," she murmured.

He made a guttural noise when she said his name. Her hands went through his hair and ran through the silky strands. His tongue danced with hers and she yanked his head down with his hair when the fire he lit made her burn from the inside out.

She was so wet it made her thighs slick with the moisture. Adelina clenched her legs as the emptiness became nearly unbearable. She'd wanted this for so long that all it took was a heated kiss and she felt ready for him. When he broke the kiss to trail his lips down her neck and bite the soft skin of her shoulder she gasped. He pressed his hips against hers at the small sound she made.

"This is why I can never let you touch me in public," he growled in her ear. "You make me lose control."

She shivered at his words and the feel of his breath on her bare skin. One of his hands caressed her bare hip, up her ribcage until he was at her breast. Just before he touched her he drew away and Adelina couldn't allow that. She pressed herself into him and he groaned as her breast filled his hand.

Alpha's breathing was ragged as he gripped her tight with one hand and gently stroked the top of her breast with the other. His fingers trailed down the skin of her stomach. His eyes found hers and she nodded in response to his unspoken question. Alpha kissed her hard, tongue in her mouth to taste and explore as he ripped the lacy fabric apart to expose her.

Her nipples were hard against the cold dawn and she couldn't help the small moan as his thumb stroked the tender flesh. The sensation overwhelmed her and she wanted more as the ache grew. Adelina needed him to touch her.

Her small hand went to his much larger one on her hip. Slowly she moved it as he kissed her senseless.

Chest heaving with each ragged breath as he slowly took her mouth, trailing his tongue over her lips, nibbling them, and taking such care with her as if he had all the time in the world to learn exactly how she tasted – she wrapped one leg around Alpha's waist to reveal her swollen sex.

Alpha's hand trembled ever so slightly as she placed it between her legs. She released him and bit his bottom lip as she waited for him to decide what to do next. She'd given him the permission and she rolled her hips against his, showing him she was sure she wanted it.

His hesitant fingers brushed her clit so softly he almost didn't touch her at all, but it sent a spark through her. Adelina sighed with pleasure, but she needed more. She briefly lifted her hips to his and felt the hardness of his cock against her sex. She moaned into his lips and Alpha growled. His fingers pressed softly against her clit, his thumb stroking it as his other rubbed and rolled her nipple. The combined sensation sent a streak of lightning through her.

With another moan she dug her fingernails into his shoulders as he stroked with the same patience he kissed her with. Her guard knew exactly what he was doing and Adelina loved it.

She lifted her hips to give him better access and the hand on her breast trailed down to her wet center. He stroked her outer lips as his thumb continued the same continuous pressure with each slow movement. It drove her mad when she wanted faster and harder.

One of his large fingers dipped into her ever so slightly and she couldn't help the loud groan of pleasure as she dragged her nails down his arms, bucking against his hand with no self-control whatsoever. She had wanted this – had wanted him for too long to take this slow.

"Yes, please," she whispered as his finger slid into her again, stroking her with reverence.

His head dipped down with her pleading request and

he licked her breast as his finger entered her completely until she could feel his palm against her. His thumb continued to stroke, applying just enough pressure.

"Oh gods," she moaned as he took her nipple into his mouth. She could feel her wetness dripping all over his hands. Alpha slowly removed his finger before plunging it back in only a fraction faster.

It made her feel needy and desperate. Adelina wanted him to give her the release she'd been denied in the maze. The pressure against her skin was so taut she knew she would soon burst. A second finger entered her and he pressed against a spot inside that made everything tremble.

Adelina couldn't help the way she rode his hand, trying to get him to increase the tempo with his thumb.

His mouth on her nipple made her eyes roll into the back of her head and her legs shake. Gently he removed his fingers from her pussy and she moaned in protest. His hands grabbed her ass and hoisted her up. She wrapped her other leg around him and kissed his neck as her guard moved her to the center of the bed and she barely held on.

He laid her down and covered her body with his briefly as he gave her a kiss that drove her utterly wild. Adelina ripped his shirt apart and the sound of the fabric tearing gave her immense satisfaction. Her hands ran over the toned muscles of his chest. She wanted to lick him from head to toe, but Alpha had other things in mind.

The way he looked at her made Adelina breathless

and he went to his knees in front of her. Her eyes widened in shock when his hands went to her thighs and gently pushed them apart so she was completely and utterly exposed to him.

Goose-pimples rose on her legs from the cool air that whispered through the room from the open window. The moons shone down on them and the way it caught strands of golden brown in his hair fascinated her, but not as much as the way he pulled her forward.

His lips touched the slick wetness of her clit and she jolted from the strange feeling. Alpha paused for a moment to look up at her in question.

Adelina had no sexual experience at all and had always wondered what this might be like. She had never had someone's mouth on her before, but suddenly it was all she wanted. She *needed* to feel the way he tasted her, the warmth of his tongue...all thoughts ran out of her head when he sensed that need and licked her from the bottom of her slit to the top, long and slow. His tongue was flat against her, taking everything until he reached her clit and gave it a gentle flick with the tip his tongue.

Adelina's hands went to his head and she barely held on as the pressure built to a near unbearable sensation. Her skin felt tight and feverish and she knew she was close. Alpha put his whole mouth over her clit and stroked her hard and slow.

The warm wetness of his mouth and how soft and velvety it felt against her made her crazy. She pressed herself against him and the tightness came down on her like a net.

A thick finger entered her and Adelina threw her head back with a cry, her hips rolling, riding his mouth as she felt the pressure about to burst. Alpha groaned against her and the vibration was exquisite. His finger plunged in and out of her faster, keeping up with the motion of her hips.

She cried out his name as she finally found her release. The waves of pleasure made her shiver but he didn't let go. He kept his fingers inside her while he licked her long and slow. The intense sensation had her legs quivering as she moaned his name. Her limbs were useless.

Alpha grinned up at her and started to undo his pants. He pushed them down slowly as she watched. Adelina licked her lips.

"Was that what you wanted?" he asked her huskily. His rock-hard cock sprang free from the fabric and Adelina felt the emptiness inside – like she was starved for him.

She grabbed Alpha and pulled him down on top of her. "You are exactly what I wanted." His hard length pressed against her and she soaked him with her wetness. Alpha bit her lip and couldn't keep from growling as she reached down to wrap her hand around him.

"I want you to take me," she demanded, squeezing gently for emphasis. "I want you to have my virginity, freely given with love." Adelina licked his bottom lip and nibbled softly when his hands spasmed on her waist.

His eyes were dark with lust and he nodded. Alpha gently pulled back and allowed her to guide him. The tip of his cock pressed against her entrance and Adelina moaned at the sensation. She was so wet the resistance was nothing but sweet torture as he slowly pushed into her. That awful feeling of emptiness abated as his hips finally met hers and he filled her completely; stretching her.

Adelina threw her head back as he slowly pulled out and then pushed back in. The sensation was almost more than she could bear, but she wanted it. She wanted him to take her harder and faster.

Gripping Alpha's hips hard she dug in and pulled him against her every time he drew out. As the pain dissipated the pleasure mounted hard and fast. Adelina whispered his name, begging him silently to take his fill of her.

Alpha's breathing grew ragged as he pumped in and then out, increasing his tempo against his will it seemed. He leaned down and kissed her hard enough to bruise. Adelina dug her nails into his ass.

"More," she whispered.

It was his undoing. Alpha groaned and obeyed. He shuddered into her one last time right as she felt the pleasure burst like molten fire. She screamed and felt herself clench around his pulsing cock. The feel of his hot seed inside made her shiver.

Adelina held on tight as Alpha roared when his orgasm gripped him. He collapsed against her once he was spent as she shuddered and pulsed around him, milking every last drop from his body.

Stroking his hair she slowly caught her breath, feeling

drowsy and languorous. Alpha lifted his head up and gave her soft sweet kisses as he murmured his adoration against her skin. He rolled them over and Adelina rested her head against his chest. She enjoyed the feel of him against her and inside of her.

Before she knew it she was fast asleep.

~

When Adelina woke up, the bright Kala sun streamed into her room from the open window and Alpha's cock was still inside of her. She gasped as he slowly, so slowly pulled out. His tip pressed against her lower lips and his hands ran up her thighs, already rock hard. Adelina couldn't help the way she scored his back with her fingernails.

Their lovemaking was much quicker than the night before, but no less passionate. He took her gently and Adelina cried out against him as he stroked in and out.

Her orgasm rippled through her and it sent him over the edge. Alpha pressed his hips against hers hard as his seed filled her. It was enough to make her scream again as another wave of pleasure hit her and overtook her senses.

Alpha kissed her and Adelina lost herself in his scent and taste. The way he surrounded her made her feel safe and loved in a way she had never experienced before and she wanted more of it.

Then he got up and smiled at her before disappearing into her washroom. A few moments later she heard the water turn on.

Rolling onto her stomach she rested her head on her pillowed arms with a smile. If she could wake up every day like this she would be happy. From the floating glass spheres above her nightstand it was later in the morning than she normally woke up, but still before her scheduled *ai-kuda* lessons with Alpha and her sisters.

Adelina ticked off what she would need to do that morning in her head while she listened to Alpha wash. She had half a mind to join him, but she wanted to enjoy the lazy and sated sensation just a little while longer.

Her simulcast went off at the same time the water did. Adelina reached for it and managed to brush it with her fingertips, coaxing it towards her. She pressed her finger against the plas-glass and the device lit up with an emergency code.

Instantly Adelina was up and her mind clear of the sexual fog she'd been enjoying.

Footage from the Khara System was all over the newsfeeds and her mouth dropped open in horror as she watched the royal family butchered by a race she could only assume was the Neprijat per the whispers she'd had her ear to for the last few months.

The recorder zoomed in as the crowned one sliced a chunk of skin from one of the young princesses. He chewed the flesh with delight as he raped her from behind.

Her simulcast dropped to the floor and shattered in a million pieces. Adelina retched and everything still in her stomach splashed against the plush carpet of her room.

Suddenly Alpha was by her side, holding her and

rubbing her back. He said comforting words she couldn't hear through the ringing in her ears.

Adelina knew the royal family of Khara. They'd had longstanding peace for decades and decades. She'd played with the princesses in their gardens and then hers cycles later. The king and queen had been kind and generous. The oldest prince, despite the age difference, had ridden with them through the royal forests.

The news stated the entire royal family had been slaughtered that way. The youngest prince, an acquaintance since childhood, was missing but the Neprijat hunted him. Her heart pounded and Adelina couldn't think straight.

Alpha stopped rubbing her back for a moment and his eyes took on a faraway look. The implanted simulcast all guards had must have alerted him. He tapped his temple and agreed to whatever orders he'd been given.

"Lina, my love..." Alpha looked her over and shook his head. He took her in his arms and carried her into the washroom. Carefully he drew a bath for her and placed her in the huge tub. He stepped in and pulled her back against him.

With his arms wrapped around her Adelina felt protected. Her entire body shook with the shock and horror.

"Varan got me proof of their existence just last night, how could this happen so quickly?" she asked, her voice barely above a whisper. Adelina couldn't comprehend what she'd seen.

Alpha said nothing as he absorbed the meaning of her

words. He pressed his lips to her neck. "I don't know," he said gruffly. The sight must have affected him as well. His entire body was rigid.

"They're going to come for us next," Adelina whispered. She stared out the huge window of her washroom to the gorgeous day outside that felt so at odds with the chill deep inside her bones.

"Not if I have anything to say about it," Alpha growled, holding her tighter. He was silent for a moment. "The royal family is convening. They want your presence within the hour. All but the announcement is cancelled today."

Adelina nodded dumbly. The youngest, Prince Nash, might still be alive – but it was doubtful he would stay that way. The ramifications of that shook her. Peace was no longer guaranteed and it seemed they were on the brink of war for the first time in centuries.

"I'm afraid," she admitted quietly. Sound felt vulgar after what she'd seen. "If they come for us I will take my own life before I allow that to happen to me."

Alpha stroked her hair. "I swear on my honor, Lina. I will never let them do that to you. I would kill you before they could even touch you."

She sagged with relief.

Her guard would keep her safe. The male she loved would protect her. He'd given her an oath.

"It is time I step back into my world," she said with regret. Adelina had to put her crown back on and be a princess once more. She turned and kissed Alpha one last time before the day begun. "Will you come back tonight?" she asked, half afraid he would say no.

Alpha pressed his forehead against hers. "I will come back for as long as you will have me."

His words made her smile despite everything.

Adelina climbed out of the tub and stood under the *nila*. "Then I expect to see you." She selected the style and watched him eye her from the tub.

He nodded in acquiescence.

"I need to speak with my father and sister about this horror," Adelina told him. "And see what their plan of action is."

7

ADELINA

Announcements Balcony
Draga Royal Palace
Planet Draga Terra

Adelina was furious.

She clenched her hands into fists and tried not to glare with the recorders on her. Her father and sister had decided to do *nothing*. There would be no retribution for their allies and friends.

It may be the smart choice, but it was also a cowardly one.

Waiting for the moment she was supposed to walk across the balcony and join her family, Adelina made sure her face was nothing more than a blank, polite mask even though her skin felt flushed with her fury and her jaw was clenched tight enough her teeth might crack.

The announcement from her father was only

moments away. She stood tall with her hands clasped in front of her and a small smile on her face. It had never felt more false than it did right then.

The king and queen had already crossed the massive palace balcony facing the city to take their thrones

Each and every announcement and appearance by the royal family was broadcasted to every livestream and cast. Citizens would be watching on their simulcasts and their viewers in their homes if they weren't attending as nobles, already seated behind the thrones or down in the streets with the rest of the capitol.

Raena crossed when she was announced. She stalked across the marble and stared down the crowd. She didn't smile and she curtseyed with her head up. It was an impressive show of spirit and dominance. Raena smiled when the crowd cheered wildly. The people loved her and they had no idea how drastically everything was about to change.

The horror of the vid was gossip on everyone's lips but the Khara System was far away and easy to forget if they wished. It was a fact that made Adelina's nails dig into her palms hard enough to break the skin. The tang of Adelina's blood on the air was noticeable only to her.

Giselle was demure in comparison to Raena, but she waved – something she loved to do simply because it irritated their grandmother. More cheers as she sat to Raena's left. Each of the smaller thrones was lined up slightly behind the king and queen; three daughters on the queen's side and three sons on the king's.

Nerves broiled in Adelina's stomach. She hated this part.

A broadcast always made her so nervous. The attention was heavy and she was under constant scrutiny. Adelina always feared she would do something atrocious on a livestream and would never be able to live down the embarrassment.

Then her name was called. She would have thought after so many cycles she would be used to it by now, but it was just as horrible each time. Her hands shook and she kept them clasped tight as she crossed.

Alpha caught her eye and she felt the anger cool slightly when he smiled at her. Adelina's smile widened when the people cheered for her as well. Her curtsey was deep and graceful, eyes downcast. She kept repeating her dance teacher's words as she held the precarious position a second longer than was required.

When she sat in her chair she slowly let out the breath she'd been holding so no one could see her anxiety, not even the recorder.

Her brothers' announcements flew by and it wasn't until her father stood before his people she was able to quiet the roar in her ears. Her heart pounded as though she'd run for hours and hours, but with the submissives' breathing exercises she was able to remain calm.

Her father's advisor stood as well and joined the king at the banister, a few steps behind as usual. "Thank you for attending," King Orion's voice boomed across the city streets with the amplifier activated. He planted both hands on the rail and he looked strong and sure. No one would have guessed he was ill if they weren't already aware.

"I have been diagnosed with hypomalarya and as such will be retiring earlier than expected." King Orion had a way with the truth. His simple and direct approach had earned him the love and respect of trillions. He always spoke to them as if they were equals.

The king had a deep respect for his people and never assumed their work was unimportant. It was the most valuable thing he'd taught Raena in Adelina's opinion. Without their citizens everything would come to a screeching halt and it was wise not to forget that.

Adelina kept her eyes on her hands but slid her glance over to Giselle, who held perfectly still, and Raena next to her. Raena looked out at the crowd without the slightest wrinkle on her forehead. She may be panicking on the inside, but she had a cool and serene exterior; her lack of fear would bolster the people during the difficult transition.

"My heir, Princess Raena will be crowned Queen of Draga two weeks after Princess Adelina's coming-of-age and I invite you all to attend the coronation of your new queen." Their father turned and held out his hand for Raena. She rose gracefully and crossed to his side, taking his hand respectfully before curtseying again.

The king's advisor scanned his simulcast. Questions had to be flooding in from the public. Even the nobles looked restless and Adelina's anxiety skyrocketed. They'd expected a commotion but the feeling in the air was almost hostile rather than confused

She glanced back at Alpha standing at attention behind the thrones with the other royal guards. He looked distracted and his gaze faraway. There had to be chatter on his internal simulcast.

"Questions from the public have come in on the livestream," the advisor said loud and clear for all to hear. "The overwhelming majority want to know, why so soon? How can the crown princess possibly be ready so many cycles before she was scheduled to reign?"

The king smiled at the crowd and then Raena as though the question didn't bother him. "Hypomalarya is an aggressive disease with no known cure. It is best Princess Raena take over sooner rather than later." The reasons why fell heavy on Adelina's mind. "Over the next six months she will slowly take over one step at a time. Now would be the perfect moment to ease some of your concerns. Princess Raena will answer the remainder of the questions."

The king bowed to his eldest daughter and returned to his throne. Raena would be required to answer every question for the next fifteen minutes and Adelina couldn't imagine the stress of it all. Raena never once wavered. Each question she answered with a clear and logical response.

Finally her time was up and she placed her hands on the banister as their father had. Her closing statement would send the people either against her, or for her. "My father, the king, has done an admirable job for Draga. He has kept the peace and ensured the citizens of our system and kingdom have voices. He has ensured that our vast resources are available to everyone and I intend on continuing his legacy. I was trained by the best, and plan to prove that to you all." She curtseyed deep and the crowd cheered despite the flurry of questions and comments Adelina could feel on her simulcast in her pocket.

The second Raena sat down there was an explosion.

Heat burned the air and screams echoed against the marble. The blast threw Adelina to the ground and the balcony cracked beneath her. She grasped for purchase, not quite able to believe what was happening.

Nobles ran and the guards were everywhere. Adelina couldn't find the source of the explosion. She tried to get to her feet and another blast rocked the palace hard enough to make her fall.

Adelina tried to break her fall but the marble was cold and hard. Pain shot up her wrist and she rolled towards the banister. The balcony's cracks spider-webbed until they reached the palace itself. She tried to find her parents, her siblings – there was so much chaos and so many people running Adelina couldn't focus.

Someone screamed her name as she tried to get up but collapsed from the pain in her wrist.

A loud crack resounded and Adelina felt it in her bones right before the entire slab of marble underneath her started to shift. As she slid Adelina realized what was happening.

Again she tried to get to her feet, but her wrist wouldn't hold her weight and she fell. The bones had to be broken even though she couldn't feel the full extent of the pain yet.

Adelina cradled her wrist to her chest and looked up to try and find anyone who could help her. Her father and mother were ushered off the marble balcony despite her mother's protests.

Once again her dual roles as queen and mother split with no regard to emotions. Her children were missing and there was nothing she could do about it.

Where was Alpha?

Adelina placed one hand on the floor and kicked off her shoes. Her bare feet were able to hold on to the slick marble better and she pushed herself towards the palace. She was so slow and the rumble of the stone beneath her was ominous.

She heard her name again and looked up. Giselle reached out to her, but her own guard carted her off like a wild animal, kicking and screaming. Adelina almost smiled at her sister's bravery.

Another shudder below made her refocus. Adelina was so far from the rest of them and the angle of the balcony grew steeper. The guards rushed for equipment to get the rest of them to safety.

A female a few meters from Adelina sobbed as she tried to hold onto a large crack. She recognized the girl. She was a Deytis, a lady with no guard of her own. Adelina shuffled over to her and murmured words of encouragement.

The girl was frozen with fear.

"Lora," Adelina snapped. "You will die here if you do

not move." Finally the girl looked up at the stern words and nodded through her tears. Gods she was so young. "Good girl, Lora. Climb up and stick to the sides."

With any luck pieces would crumble and fall, not the entire slab of marble.

The two made their way from crack to crack as the balcony continued to break apart, shattering against the ground so far below them. If there was another explosion Adelina knew she wouldn't be able to make it, not with only one good arm.

Where was Alpha? He should have been by her side seconds after the initial explosion and she couldn't find him in the chaos. Had they reassigned him during the emergency?

Screams from the crowd below reached her and Adelina had to catch her breath. Her gown was ripped and her wrist hurt worse than she could ever remember. Lora looked back down and hesitated.

"Keep going," Adelina urged. "Find someone and get help."

The girl nodded and climbed as though she were born to it. Orders from a princess motivated her and Adelina was glad she could help one person at least.

Her arm started to tremble as she held on and she didn't think she would make it to safety. The balcony wouldn't hold for much longer and she couldn't climb such a steep incline with only one hand.

She rested her sweaty forehead against the cold marble. Her breath was shaky and the smell of the explosive was thick in the air among the dust.

"Lina!" Alpha's voice reached her and her gaze snapped to his.

He wasn't far. Alpha jumped over rubble and slid across the slick floor towards her. The biggest crack in the marble separated them and it wouldn't be long before the heavy weight of the balcony over nothing but air would deepen the fracture until it could no longer support the weight.

"Lina, grab my hand and climb up!" Alpha reached out towards her and he was frantic. He'd disobeyed protocol and wasn't even wearing safety gear or a tether to pull them back up.

"I can't!" Adelina yelled. "My wrist is broken, Alpha. I can't climb any farther."

She could take his hand but he would have to bear the full brunt of her weight and then pull her up. Without a tether Alpha could slip and fall, taking them both down.

"I can hold you, just take my hand." His blue eyes pleaded with hers and they both knew the risk. There was a good chance he couldn't.

Would she risk his life? Did she really have a choice? It was take the risk or die...and Adelina wasn't ready for her own death.

"I'm going to jump towards you and reach out..." she trailed off. The screaming and yelling a constant background and the balcony shifted again. It was now or never.

"I'll catch you," he promised.

Adelina closed her eyes for a brief second and took a

breath. She trusted Alpha with her life. He would keep his word.

She pushed off with her legs, using every bit of strength she had and reached out with her good hand.

There was a moment where she was suspended and weightless – a moment where she doubted. Then Alpha's strong hands caught hers and gravity came down hard. Adelina slammed against the marble and the breath was knocked out of her. She looked up and Alpha strained, his feet braced and then he pulled. Adelina felt herself rise. He'd done it.

There was a percussive wave before the sound of another explosion hit her. The marble shifted and fell and Adelina felt her hand slide out of Alpha's. He pitched forward and they slipped. The sensation in her stomach had her panicking, scrabbling for purchase – for anything she could get her hands on.

Adelina screamed as she fell backwards.

Their fall was halted abruptly and they both slammed into the marble floor as nobles and guards ran for safety. Alpha had managed to catch a large crack in the marble, his hand wedged in deep.

He had kept his promise.

Alpha's hand held hers so hard it hurt and she could feel the bones grind together. He pulled her up with one arm, a testament to his new strength, and she used the arm of her broken wrist to hold her place as she let go of Alpha. Adelina wedged her own hand into the crack and looked to Alpha for direction. She said nothing, but her eyes were wide and she knew she looked frightened. They were both stranded.

"It's going to be okay, Lina. I'll get us out of this." Alpha pressed his forehead to hers gently and she nodded. She trusted him implicitly.

Alpha planted his feet against the marble and pulled himself up. The crack was wide enough he could stand on it. The skill of the architects the only reason the entire balcony hadn't fallen to the ground far below them already. But his weight on the edge made the entire slab shudder.

"Alpha," Adelina warned. "It's about to fall." She could feel it beneath her as it slowly came apart at the seams.

Without a word he grabbed her under the arms and pulled as hard as he could. Adelina flew upwards and the marble gave way beneath them. Alpha jumped back with her and then scrabbled backwards as fast as he could, pulling her along the whole way. Adelina held her tongue as she bore the pain in her wrist.

Alpha got them both back behind the huge archway between the palace and the balcony and they watched as the entire thing split off and plummeted. Huge chunks slammed into the earth and marble broke through buildings. Adelina only hoped most of their people had gotten away in time.

They both breathed heavily and Adelina turned into him, resting her head against his chest. Alpha held her tight, his arms around her, pulling her into his lap as he leaned against the arch. "I thought I'd lost you," he muttered over and over. "I couldn't find you, Lina, and I thought you were dead." Alpha buried his face in her dusty hair and she gripped him tight with her good hand.

"You found me," she tried to soothe. "I'm okay. You saved me."

Adelina wanted to tell him how much she loved him. She wanted to tell him everything she'd been meaning to put into words. She stroked his hair and kissed him hard – protocol and the recorders be damned. Adelina wouldn't be alive if it weren't for him.

"Lina!" Giselle's screech was a slap back into reality. Her sister threw herself on Adelina and inspected every bit of her. Adelina hissed when she touched her arm.

"You need to see a physician right away," Giselle scolded. "The guards are investigating the explosion, but a male was caught and he's being questioned now. It won't be long before we have answers."

Giselle helped Adelina up and Alpha stood slowly as her sister dragged her away. Adelina looked back at her guard and tried to tell him with one look everything she felt. She promised herself she would find him later and tell him.

8

ADELINA

Council Room
Draga Royal Palace
Planet Draga Terra

Adelina's arm was in a sling and she had been required to have help cleaning up and dressing. It was a bit humiliating, but the maid had been excited and flattered to be chosen to assist a princess. Adelina hadn't wanted to ruin it for her by complaining. Instead she had thanked her and let her fuss over the broken bones and bruises.

It hadn't even been an hour since the incident and Adelina had received a cast calling her to the council room. The entire royal family was there including the Queen Mother – her grandmother. Advisors and nobles also crowded the room. A few heads of guilds and the Mistress of the House of Kismet herself.

Adelina couldn't tear her eyes from the gorgeous courtesan's figure.

The courtesans were such a mystery – so sexual. The mistress caught her stare and winked at Adelina. She blushed and looked down, embarrassed to have been caught. Only a few more months and the mistress would assign her a courtesan to train her. Adelina wondered who she would choose.

A male cleared his throat behind her. Guards lined the walls of the council room and Adelina spotted Alpha among them. He stared forward, not acknowledging if he saw her or not. She turned back to her father and tried not to let it bother her.

"We've captured one of the bombers and our interrogators have relayed he is a mercenary, part of a team which we are currently on the hunt for," King Orion stated, eyes narrowed and voice harsh. He was furious and it showed. Every muscle in his face was tense and the tendons in his neck corded as he ground his teeth together. "These males seem to have been hired by a noble family, and the reason has yet to be uncovered."

Their own nobles plotted against them? The last time there was a plot against the throne from their own people was hundreds of cycles ago. The prospect sent chills up and down Adelina's spine. She couldn't imagine not being able to trust the people who surrounded her.

She glanced at the different nobles and a few of them shifted uncomfortably. Adelina took note of whom.

"I suspect this may have something to do with who

Raena may choose as her partner. As such we will have a Choosing Call and invite the entire system. By the coronation Raena will have chosen a husband. An heir will be imminent and the future secure." The king sighed and looked to his eldest.

Raena nodded and stepped forward. Adelina watched her closely for signs of how she felt about the situation. "I do not take this choice lightly, and will choose based on my own will and no one else's. This will secure my reign as queen and fulfill part of my duty to the realm." She met every single noble's gaze and held it. There would be no question who would be the one choosing, who would be the sole ruler of Draga.

Raena was determined, she was brave and there were no doubts on her face or in her eyes. Adelina caught the mistress smiling, a proud look Adelina didn't quite understand. She noted it and reminded herself to write it down later. The mistress was an ally, but there was more to it than that. She would find out what.

The murmurs of the nobles and advisors grew so loud they turned to shouts. Finally Raena put a stop to it. "Silence!" She glared until they all shut their mouths. Every single one of them looked surprised they'd felt compelled to obey. Adelina smiled. The Draga genes were not to be trifled with.

"Do any of you have a disagreement with this decision the king and I have made?" Without the help of their advisors it seemed.

None of them spoke. There were plenty of single

courtiers who undoubtedly planned to approach her at a later time, on their own.

One of the older advisors cleared her throat; the Lord High Admiral Tamika inclined her head to the chief advisor, Caspian, in deference and then spoke. "Do you believe, Princess Raena, it is wise to lose such a strong bargaining chip before ascending to the throne?"

It was a fair question and Adelina agreed it seemed rather hasty.

Raena seemed to concur, but she'd made her decision and would stick to it. "An heir of my own is more important."

Giselle was loved by the people, but she was never meant to be a queen and Goddess protect Raena, but if she were to die Giselle would not be a good choice. The people loved her reckless ways and her fighting spirit, but those weren't traits they'd want in their queen. Someone trained, someone dependable, someone who would value them more than their own desires was what they needed. Raena's heir would be trained for nothing less.

Tamika seemed to understand the sacrifice. She bowed to Raena. "No further questions, your highness."

The room was silent and she gave them five more seconds before cutting off any further questions. "The invitations will be sent out and there will be no announcement. We cannot afford a public display at the moment. The livestream will have to be satisfied with daily court life for the time being, and we will attempt to make them more personal until we can tighten our security and find the culprits." Raena stepped back and allowed the king to take the spotlight once again.

"My best people will continue the investigation into how the mercenaries managed to get so close without tripping any of our highly sensitive alarms. It points to inside help, and as you all know the crime is treason and an attempt to murder a member of the royal family, not to mention the deaths of innocent civilians." The king's dark gaze sent every single person's eyes to the floor.

There was a reason everyone respected the king.

He dismissed them all and Adelina kept her eye on Alpha. She hadn't gotten a chance to talk to him since the chaos. The guards were always the last to file out so she left with the rest of her family and waited outside the council room door.

The bright sunlight streaming in from the floor to ceiling windows belied the aura of despair she could still feel after the bombings.

Adelina breathed the clean air in deep. The robotics had already cleaned the dust from the air and currently worked on repairing the balcony as suspects were interrogated. The guards filed out in a precise march and split off to their scheduled areas. An entire group of them headed towards the security wing and the guardhouse. Adelina spotted Alpha among them and followed.

She didn't want to call out his name and embarrass him in front of his comrades. Adelina took her new simulcast out of her pocket and sent him a quick message. Adelina saw him check his personal device and slip it back into his pocket.

Alpha continued on with the other guards and didn't slow his pace. Adelina frowned. Was he purposefully ignoring her communication? She sent another message asking him to meet her in the study and turned abruptly.

The stairs were down the hall and she couldn't stop thinking the whole way there if something had happened between the incident and now. It was such a short time, had someone spoken to him? Had Alpha been scolded or punished for his familiar treatment of her?

Everyone knew how close they were, it was doubtful he'd be punished for saving her life no matter how he did it.

The royal study was empty and Adelina relaxed just a little. No recorders were allowed in the study and her entire family was busy with the aftermath of the bombings. William had orders as a warrior, and Giselle did also as a volunteer. Asher had his training and Ian his science. Raena had an entire system to rule in a few short months.

Once again Adelina was forgotten. She didn't mind really, but occasionally she wished she could do more to help. It's why she quietly gathered information. Intel was invaluable and she could use it to advise her sister. It was why she secretly went out disguised aside from her own desires. Until her wrist healed she would be stuck inside the palace walls.

Then she would go out and help her people.

Adelina sat on a window seat and watched the guards scurry over the palace grounds. Triple the normal amount of security patrolled the area and she assumed the entire capitol.

She played with the soft spidersilk of her gown and tried to imagine the changes such an event would have on her life. An assassination from a neighboring system and kingdom was to be expected, but a bombing that put innocent lives in danger from one of their own people? It was difficult to fathom.

This placation of a royal wedding would only do so much. The real source of the malice would need to be found and fixed. Adelina would have to do some digging if she were to help her sister.

Who would be the best to speak to? Her mind went to the courtesans, but their confidentiality agreement would hinder her. Perhaps there was a way around it. They engaged with anyone who had the gold, from all walks of life. They would know anything she could think of to ask.

The door opened and she looked back to see Alpha in the doorway. His face was a blank mask and a bad feeling settled in Adelina's stomach. He was completely closed off from her and she had no idea why.

Adelina shot to her feet and crossed the room. Alpha stepped into the study and closed the door behind him. She threw her good arm around his neck and hugged him tight, her face buried in his chest.

"Is something wrong?" Adelina asked. Her panic skyrocketed as his mask stayed in place and he kept his hands to himself. Those blue eyes she loved so much were dull and lacked the light that was there every time he looked at her. "Are you hurt?" she demanded.

Alpha shook his head. "No, I'm not hurt Princess. Thank you for asking."

A knife twisted in her heart and she took a step back from him. Something was very wrong. "Alpha, I asked you to meet with me because I wanted to tell you how grateful I am that you were there to save me. Without you I doubt I'd be standing here right now," she told him, placing a hand on his cheek. He had to know how she felt. "You have to know how much I care for you." Adelina was such a coward. She shook her head. No, she didn't just care for him, it was more than that.

Alpha took her hand and removed it from his face. "I appreciate what you're trying to do, Princess."

Her title felt like a slap. "You know you may call me by my given name. What's wrong?"

"I can't," was all he said. He dropped her hand and clasped his hands behind his back.

Adelina could feel the knife twisting harder, deeper and she gasped for air. What had changed so drastically and so quickly? "What do you mean you can't?" she snapped. The way he acted triggered a fury she didn't know she had. "You can't *what* exactly?"

Alpha flinched at the tone in her voice. Adelina never raised her voice – ever. "I can't continue a romantic relationship with you, Princess."

Even though by that point she expected the words, they still hurt worse than anything she could remember, including the punishment she'd had.

"Why not? You owe me an explanation at the very least. Not an hour ago you held me in your arms as though you loved me." Tears pricked Adelina's eyes and she hated them. "Do my feelings not matter? Do you not care that I love you?" There, she'd finally said it, but she'd spat the words out like a bad taste in her mouth.

Finally he looked down at her. His eyes met hers directly and they pleaded with her, they begged her not to make this worse. "Lina, please, you almost died today and I wasn't there until it was almost too late."

He finally unclasped his hands and took her in his arms. He rested his head on top of hers and breathed her in. "Everything about you distracts me, your taste, your smell, the small smile you save only for me."

The tears finally fell, streaking her cheeks and she didn't even bother to wipe them away. Alpha had made his choice. She could hear it in his voice and feel it in the way he held her.

"If I hadn't been so busy staring at you, maybe I would have seen something suspicious sooner, perhaps I could have stopped them before they could set off the bombs. Then you wouldn't be here with a broken wrist and scratches on your beautiful face." He pulled back and traced the marks gently. "I cannot afford another mistake like that, not when it is your life on the line. You're too important to me, Lina."

Alpha kissed her cheek and then took another step back. "I would understand if you want me reassigned."

When Adelina looked up into his face his stare was blank yet again.

She was a royal Draga, she reminded herself.

Adelina straightened and clasped her hands in front of her, head held high as though she currently wore the crown she was born to. "I do not accept your offer for reassignment, Guard."

Adelina was proud of herself. The words didn't get stuck in her throat and she sounded strong and sure rather than the heartbroken fool she was. She shoved her emotions down deep to deal with later. At the moment a guard needed her direction, and that was all he was to her right now.

"I will not punish you for a mistake that I have made. You have earned your position as my royal guard. You are dismissed."

Her cold words fractured the bored look on his face briefly as he studied her. Then he slipped it back on and bowed before exiting the study.

The second he was gone Adelina's hand went to her stomach and she gasped. The pain was unexpected and the depth of it seemed unending. How anyone survived heartbreak was beyond her. Adelina wanted nothing more to do with it.

She had been such a fool to think Alpha would ever give up his position as guard – a position he had worked so hard for – even for her. If he had fully accepted her love for him then it would have occurred to him he could not be her guard forever, but all he could see were his failings – how she would distract him in the future rather than her hiring a new guard to take his place, because then Alpha would have the royal title of prince.

Adelina had to talk to someone. She sat on the window bench and tried to catch her breath.

She would find someone she could talk to the second she stopped crying.

9

ADELINA

King's Quarters
Draga Royal Palace
Planet Draga Terra

Adelina knocked softly on her father's door. His worn voice reached her through the thick wood and she pressed her hand against the frame. There was a click as it unlocked and she opened it slowly. Her father was seated in his sitting room with a blanket across his lap in front of the fireplace, despite how warm it was.

There was tea and food on the table beside him, but he had a book in his hand instead. He looked up when she entered and smiled warmly. "Come join me," her father said.

Adelina kept her eyes down as she crossed the room and sat in the chair next to him, facing the roaring fire. It felt hot on her skin, but she ignored it. Her father studied her and then he frowned. Suddenly he was the king.

"Tell me what happened," he demanded, setting his book down on the table harder than necessary. The delicate china rattled and Adelina winced.

"I wanted to ask for your advice," she said, twisting her skirts in her good hand.

Her father was the perfect person to talk to. He would understand what she needed. King Orion loved his queen more than anything, and he loved his mistress as well. The three of them got along better than most wedded couples Adelina had seen in court. Her father would know what she did wrong, and what to do in the future.

"Alpha just ended our relations."

Her father growled in anger and threw the blanket off his lap.

Adelina sprang to her feet, placing her good hand on his chest to stop him from tearing the male to pieces. "Please," she begged. Father was wildly protective of his children, and if she didn't handle him carefully, Alpha would end up somewhere awful. "Let me tell you why."

When her father looked at her the lines on his face eased and he let out an exasperated sigh as he sat down. "Of course child, I will listen before I make any rash decisions."

"Thank you." Adelina dragged her chair closer to him so she could hold his hand and reassure him. She sat delicately and rearranged her skirts, nervous as her mother would usually be the one to have this conversation with her.

"Child, tell me quickly or I will decide on my own," he warned.

Adelina let out a breath and gave up. She would simply spit it out then. "He declared I was too distracting and we couldn't continue the relationship due to the events of today, and that perhaps he would have been a better guard if he weren't...thinking of me."

The king sat back in his chair and watched her closely. Adelina dropped protocol. She needed answers. She looked up into her father's eyes and tried to discern what thoughts were hidden behind those dark purple depths.

"I knew there was a reason I liked that boy," he finally said.

Adelina was still too hurt to joke about the situation. She loved Alpha still. She would have to see him every single day and know he would never be hers. The pain made it difficult to breathe and she felt like she drowned in the sensation. Her eyes stayed dry though. No more tears for a male who didn't want her the same way she wanted him.

"Papa, please. I am very...upset about this."

They didn't usually talk about emotions so directly and it was uncomfortable. She shifted in her seat and leaned back. Her father squeezed her hand lovingly and gave the top a little pat before turning to pour her a cup of tea.

"I am told by your mother tea can cure almost any

ailment." He handed her the cup with a sad smile. "I know it won't make it better right away, but it will help."

He waited until she sipped before taking a breath to speak. "Alpha has always been a wonderful companion to you throughout the cycles and I have never regretted sponsoring him after his parent's death. He is honorable and dependable. He would have made an excellent prince, dear one." Father chucked her under the chin gently. "But perhaps this is a blessing."

Adelina set the teacup down. It was difficult to see how a male she was head over heels in love with – who didn't want to be with her was a good thing. She tucked her legs underneath her and focused all of her attention on her father.

"You never want to convince someone they should be with you. They will regret it eventually and start to resent you. If Alpha truly was the one for you he would have done anything to stay with you, even give up his favored guard position."

He was silent for a moment and Adelina considered his words. "Maybe it was something that hadn't occurred to him?" she asked. "I never asked him if he would give it all up for me. Perhaps he didn't think of it and thought everything would remain as it is." That would explain why he felt like they couldn't be together as princess and guard.

Her father shrugged as he looked into the crackling flames. "It is a difficult puzzle to untangle," he said. "One would think his position and his love for you could go hand in hand, yet he doesn't seem to believe so." Her father turned to her then. "He has made his decision and to try to convince or coerce him now would be fruitless. You want someone to fight for you, Lina, not against you."

It wasn't the words she wanted to hear, but he was right no matter how much the truth hurt. "I love him so much, Papa. How am I going to make it through each day while he stands by my side?"

He took her hand again and gave it a squeeze. "You will be assigned to a courtesan soon and she will help distract you," her father reminded her.

Adelina nodded as she considered the idea. Perhaps her courtesan would know what she'd done wrong, what she could have done differently. "I am excited to see the inside of the House of Kismet. Elara has never told me much and she grew up there."

The king's mistress, Elara was like a second mother to her. More like her first mother as the queen had always been extremely focused on Raena and Giselle through no fault of her own. Giselle was a handful.

The king frowned again. "The courtesan will stay with us in the palace. It is against tradition, but after the bombings I am not taking any chances with any of my children's lives."

Adelina glared at him. Without protocol and witnesses she could argue with her father and get away with it. "Papa, no. I want to see the House and do as every Draga has before me has done. I will not be coddled."

The king merely gave an exasperated sigh. "You are a very demanding female, dear one," he said with a smile.

"Don't worry; I will keep your secret." Her father gave her a wink and she couldn't help but laugh. "What about a compromise? You will be allowed to visit the first time, but then we will move the courtesan into the palace?"

It wasn't exactly what she wanted, but it was the best she would get from an over-protective father who was also king. "Thank you, Papa." Adelina gave him a kiss on the cheek. "I knew you would be able to make me feel better."

Her father always spoke the truth in a way that helped her through her murky emotions.

Losing Alpha hurt and it would for a while. Adelina was all right with that, and she would learn and grow. She would find someone who loved her in spite of her title.

Adelina would try to start fresh and perhaps rebuild the friendship she had with Alpha. Losing him as a companion would be far more painful than losing him as a lover.

"Lina would you mind painting for me?" her father asked. A wracking cough made his entire body shake and once again he looked worn down and tired.

"Of course, Papa," she replied. Adelina fetched the blanket from the floor and tucked it around her sick father. She handed him his tea and his book before taking out the painting supplies he stored for her among his shelves of books. Adelina sat near the window in her usual place and tapped her bottom lip with a pencil.

There would only be so much more time with her father like this and Adelina refused to take it for granted.

She started to sketch as she watched him closely. She hoped against all odds there would be a miracle and the scientists would find a way to give them just a little bit more time.

∽

Don't miss the rest of Draga Court with the first book in the series

Princess of Draga.

Keep flipping for the first three chapters of Princess of Draga or the international links.

PRINCESS OF DRAGA

BLURB

Princess Adelina has spent her entire life among the wolves at court, learning when to cede and when to fight, surviving the politics and intrigue. But when war comes to her galaxy an exiled prince requests sanctuary during the storm, offering what's left of his warriors.

Adelina is drawn to Prince Nash in a way she's never experienced before, but he's forbidden to her. She must decide if she will defy the Crown for a chance at love or suffer the consequences. Because war is coming and no one will remain unscathed - not even a princess.

*This is a slow burn, steamy polyamorous space fantasy romance. There is some female/female bisexual romance.

PRINCESS OF DRAGA: CHAPTER ONE

NADYAH

House of Kismet
Stella di Draga
Planet Draga Terra

Nadyah watched Lord Greyson sleep on her massive, luxurious bed. She gently brushed his hair back from his forehead and smiled softly. He was one of her favorite clients, and was always so gentle and sweet to her.

Greyson was not as dominant as he liked to pretend but Nadyah found it easy to submit to him – which was what he wanted from her. He was a good lover and never failed to ensure she had just as much pleasure as he.

As one of her favorite clients she always made time for him whenever he came to the House of Kismet.

Nadyah was the most highly respected and sought after courtesans on Draga Terra and she had a long list of clients, but who she took on was *her* choice. Courtesans always chose whom they sold their services to.

It was in her genetic makeup to enjoy her work and Nadyah thrived on the sex. She formed an emotional bond with each of her clients and they all had a small piece of her heart.

It couldn't be helped, it was in her nature.

Courtesans were the one sub-race descended from the Ancients – the Humans of old – that were neither submissive nor dominant. She was whatever her client needed her to be.

A time-keeper floated above her nightstand, it chimed softly telling her it was midnight. The sun had finally set.

Nadyah slid off the dark blue, satin sheets of her bed and padded silently across the plush carpet of her room. She reached for her spidersilk robe as she passed her vanity and wrapped the sheer material around her naked body

A backward glance at Lord Greyson lying on her massive four-poster bed confirmed he was still asleep. The outline of his body through the silk shrouds accentuated his strong shoulders. He was one of the nobility – the Marquise of the planet Priea, and he slept deeply after the hours she'd made him work.

Nadyah slipped into her closet. Beautiful gowns lined the space in various sumptuous fabrics. Shoes and accessories were displayed in a way that caught the eye and allowed her to easily choose combinations to suit her coloring.

All of her possessions were gifts from her clients. Her

income allowed for such luxuries but it was a point of pride that she wasn't required to purchase her own accoutrements.

All the way at the back of the massive closet Nadyah slid aside a few garments. Her fingertip pressed into the hidden panel and a small door slid aside noiselessly.

Waiting outside the House of Kismet was the prince of thieves. There was still a smidge of purple in the sky and the ocean breeze chilled her.

Varan turned to Nadyah and when he met her sapphire gaze her heart clenched and then began to pound in her chest. Those emerald eyes of his glittered playfully.

His broad shoulders always caught her eye without fail and every time she wondered what it would be like to be surrounded by them. Varan's tanned skin begged to be touched. The roguish smile on his face made her want to slap him even though it tantalized her.

Varan was the prince of thieves and he had stolen her heart cycles ago. Nadyah held the secret close. He had no idea how she truly felt about him and it would remain that way. She could not afford to put her position in danger.

"Nadyah," he said softly, taking her hand and dropping a kiss on it. Never once did he stare at her naked form through the sheer spidersilk robe.

She kept her face impassive despite the flutter in her heart and the feel of his lips on her skin. "Greyson is asleep. Be quick, before he wakes."

Varan's face grew serious. He nodded and went to

work. His large form grew slinky just like a deadly *galina* and he slid past her. His arm brushed against her breast and she couldn't decide if it had been on purpose or an accident.

Regardless, the touch left her breathless.

Nadyah watched him work as she leaned against the black, velvet wall. There was a reason he was the prince of all the thieves in Stella di Draga – the capitol city of Draga Terra. His fingers were light as they sifted through Lord Greyson's belongings.

The piece of tech in his hand scanned the personal devices for any possible keys and passwords. This small favor to the thief made her uncomfortable, but the stakes were high and he was an excellent source of information.

Varan's fingers moved to Greyson's hand and held it gently to be scanned and copied. Nadyah wondered what those light fingers would feel like against her own skin, trailing down her stomach...Warmth spread down her abdomen and set her skin to tingling. She felt her wetness drip onto her thighs and she pressed them together, hoping Varan wouldn't notice her arousal.

Nadyah shook her head. She needed to collect herself because Varan could never be hers.

The prince of thieves prowled across the dimly lit room towards her and his eyes flicked down her body and then up again so briefly she wasn't sure he'd actually done so.

"I'm done." His warm rumble was quieter than the Gentle God of Death.

Nadyah's nipples tightened against the soft fabric of

her robe, obvious to anyone with a set of eyes. Varan didn't react at all. Nadyah knew he figured it was all part of her position as he brushed by her once more. He couldn't be more wrong.

Varan could see her plain as day and not even a tiny reaction from him. She had wondered if he preferred males for many cycles until she saw him kissing a female in his tavern one night.

She activated the closet door with a flick of her finger to be safe. It shut behind them silently.

"Did you get what you needed?" she asked softly. She couldn't help herself. Nadyah let her hand reach for his bicep, thick with muscle. She wanted to squeeze but managed to refrain.

The hood over his head cast his face in shadow, but she could still see the emerald of his eyes practically glow in the dark. "I did get everything. Thank you, Mistress Nadyah." He tucked his scanner in a hidden pocket. "Have you heard? The royal family has sent me an invitation to their ritzy little ball." His cocky grin did wicked things to her.

Nadyah nearly crossed her arms over her chest, but she decided against it. Let him be teased. "I have not. This is a big step for you." She gave him a small smile.

The royal family didn't approve of his work as a thief, but they respected him and his position among their people. Varan took care of the citizens of Draga Terra. They were his people too as Varan would say.

"Perhaps I will see you there," Varan murmured. He tapped her bottom lip gently and then turned to the secret panel in her closet that would lead him outside and towards the ocean.

She placed a delicate hand on her hip and it pulled the sheer fabric tighter across her breasts. Nadyah arched an eyebrow. "My payment, Varan?"

The thief turned back and grinned.

Then he prowled towards her. The move was so unexpected she stepped back and he followed until he had her pressed up against the door to her room. Varan planted his hands on either side of her, so close she could smell the spicy scent of winterflowers identifying him as dominant.

His legs brushed the outside of hers, effectively trapping her between his well-muscled thighs. She smoldered where he touched her. He made her squirm and her breathing quickened when he leaned in. What in the spider's name was he doing?

His mouth found hers and he was hungry, voracious.

Her heart pounded harder in her chest and she tried not to moan aloud. He had never kissed her before. It made her want to drag her nails down his back and rip his shirt off so she could show him exactly what skills she possessed.

One of his large hands held her face gently and he nibbled on her bottom lip. Liquid fire poured from between her legs in response. She wanted him. She would take him in her closet with a client in the other room, the gods be damned.

His tongue parted her lips and he pressed his large muscled form against her body, allowing her to feel every centimeter of him. Varan's hard cock nestled between her thighs and rubbed in exactly the right place. She gasped and something hard, smooth, and round slipped into her mouth.

Varan pulled back with a grin, but it wasn't the same playful grin it was before. His eyes were too dark and hungry to be playful.

"Your payment, *milika*." He bowed before he disappeared through the secret door.

Nadyah spit the item into her palm and inspected the perfectly dark sapphire exactly the color of her eyes. Varan had left her burning from the inside out.

The sapphire went into her stash and then she opened the door to her bedroom. It was time to wake Lord Greyson and let him ease her frustrations.

Because despite how much she wanted Varan, he was the only person she could not have sex with.

~

Mistress Jael – the head of House of Kismet – summoned Nadyah the second Greyson had left sated and with promises of more diamonds.

Nadyah felt nerves coil in the pit of her stomach as she quickly made her way through the opulent House.

The thick, blood-red carpets muffled the sound of her slippers and the folds of her spidersilk gown whispered in the early morning silence. The gold embroidery of her dress caught the light of the candles that added to the romantic atmosphere of the House.

Nadyah stopped in front of the double gold-leaf doors that led to Mistress Jael's study.

Mistress Jael was not only the head of one of the most respected and revered courtesan Houses, but she was also the Spider; head of the Spymaster's Guild and Nadyah was one of her most trusted and skilled spies.

Gently the doors opened after scanning her DNA. The smoky dawn light filled the study. The candles in the Jael's study were left unlit and the Spymistress was a mere shadow at her desk.

"Please sit, darling." The Spider beckoned towards the velvet chair before the desk. Nadyah sank into the soft fabric without hesitation.

"What is it, Mistress?" Nadyah whispered. A tinge of fear tickled her spine.

Was she speaking to the Mistress of the House or the Spider?

She wondered briefly if Mistress Jael knew of her dealings with the prince of thieves. If she did, Nadyah doubted she minded.

They all had their sources of information and rarely did the Spider care how the web was woven as long as it brought her the buzzing of flies.

The smoky, silky voice wove through the room as she spoke. "There have been whispers of an assassination brewing; an enemy in the court."

Fear struck Nadyah hard and fast. Their royal family was in danger? How had she heard nothing until this moment?

The Spymistress stood and the rising sun struck her

golden hair. It glittered in the morning light. She was forty cycles old but hardly looked a day over twenty. With such an expanded lifespan each person tended to age differently and Jael did it with such magnificence.

"I am assigning you to the youngest princess, my little spider. She has finally come of age – twenty cycles old and in need of her bedroom training from only the best. You will teach her the *camerraleto* and ensure the House of Kismet's reputation is upheld."

The Spymistress glided around her desk, the picture of elegance and grace. Her soft, delicate hand briefly touched Nadyah's face in affection.

"We must protect the royal family at all costs. You are now officially a royal courtesan, Nadyah. Teach the little princess everything you know about the bedroom arts and make sure to stay close to her. Learn what you can in the palace."

"The palace, Mistress?" Nadyah was confused. Normally a royal came to the House to be taught.

"After the bombing six months ago, the king and queen have agreed it is safer if you are living in the palace for her training. Princess Adelina will visit the House just once for your initial meeting. They asked me to find their enemy and safeguard their children. You will not be the only little spider in the palace, but you will have the most freedom. Keep a sharp eye out, love." Mistress Jael bent down and brushed her lips against Nadyah's and she felt the spark between them.

Mistress Jael had spent the last ten cycles as head of

the House and rarely took a client. Still, she had not lost her skill.

It was difficult to forget Jael's touch when she had been the one to help train Nadyah since the day she was brought to the House of Kismet after her Academy training.

The two of them had been close for a long time and then things had changed when she became Mistress of the House. The distance only grew when Jael became the Spider, but Nadyah was proud of her and perhaps still a little bit in love with her.

Nadyah knew Jael's touches were platonic and all part of their life as courtesans; born and bred to be sexual. It was in their genetic makeup to be fluid in ways the rest of the races of Draga were not. They could become what society needed them to be to balance out a crowd, or even a small group of people.

She looked down at her hands as Mistress Jael turned back to her desk and rang a bell. Within seconds a servant arrived and placed a breakfast order for the two of them. The Spider made as much noise as her namesake.

Jael glided to the chair next to Nadyah, graceful and quiet as the dead. Sitting next to her rather than behind her desk meant the formal giving of orders was over.

Curious what Mistress Jael could possibly want to talk about, she waited patiently.

Nadyah was the subordinate and always the submissive in Jael's presence despite both their ability to adjust when needed. Jael looked out the massive windows behind her desk overlooking the ocean. The morning sun was weak and more yellow than its usual orange.

Rich coffee filled the room with its wondrous scent and a servant poured them both cups before placing the pot on the small table between them. Jael picked up the delicate china cup and saucer and sipped the steaming liquid carefully, choosing to drink it black. Nadyah added some sweetener and a dash of milk before drinking her own. It gave her much needed energy after a night with such little sleep.

"When will I begin the youngest princess's training?" Nadyah finally asked, breaking the silence. She lowered the cup and saucer to her lap.

Her mistress gave her a wicked smile. "She will arrive after the midday hour tomorrow."

Nadyah smiled and took another sip of her coffee. It was short notice but she looked forward to the assignment.

The Princess Adelina was a delicate little thing. She was so sweet, so demure, and loved by the people. Her black hair and lovely amethyst eyes made her more pretty than beautiful. With the right guidance she could be gorgeous.

Nadyah had seen her a few times in her life, but never up close. The pics and vids hardly did her justice per the citizens of Draga. Not much was known about this princess except she liked to read. Entire days were spent in the library or the royal study per the Spider's intel. Nadyah would have to learn more about the princess to properly do both of her jobs.

The servant returned with a small spread of fruit and nutbread. Following protocol Nadyah waited until Jael selected her food first.

Her mistress then set her coffee on the table and pulled a heavy linen card out of her dress pocket. She handed it to Nadyah before selecting a small plate of fruit.

"We have received the invitation to the royal Choosing Ball. I sent you a cast with my list of approved courtesans. Any not listed may only attend as guests of nobles. I will update you on any contracts that are made. The number of nobles who have already sent casts of their attendance is astonishing. They are coming from all over the system for this."

Mistress Jael tapped her long, sharp fingernails on the wood arm of the chair. The clicking noise seemed loud in the quiet office. "It was expected of course with all six royal children currently unwed. The most obvious choice is currently Crown Princess Raena with her upcoming coronation. Ah the prospects of being king..." she trailed off as she contemplated.

"Will the male who marries Princess Raena be king, or prince consort?" Nadyah inquired. It was an important distinction.

"He will be called king consort," Jael confirmed. "Although from what I've seen of the contract his power will be very limited."

"Has the royal family mentioned who they're

considering?" Nadyah took a small bite of warm bread and tried to keep the look of bliss off her face. The House cooks could not be rivaled.

Suddenly Nadyah was aware of the intense sexuality the Spider exuded as she leaned back in her chair, pushing her breasts out. She kept it contained mostly, but when she relaxed she became exactly what she was. Nadyah felt a flare in her belly and swallowed hard.

"So far Lord Hayden is favored to keep the peace between the families, but you know as well as I that it can be any of the nobles," Jael said. "The crown princess will be the one who has the last say though. Personally, I favor Ajax, but if Raena wanted him she would have proposed already. He's lived at court for a few cycles now."

Nadyah agreed. Ajax was a fantastic warrior and extremely handsome. He frequented the House enough they all knew of him, but he was also a cousin. It wasn't outlawed, but there were so many other options.

"Please Mistress, will you send me a list of the nobles traveling for the ball?"

"It has already been done." The Spider set her food down and stretched luxuriously; a smile on her face as though she had caught a particularly tasty fly.

"Enjoy the palace dear one, and please say hello to Elara for me. She's done well as the official mistress of the King, but I still miss having her at the House." Jael stood and her spidersilk dress became nearly see-through in the sun's light. Her fingertips brushed Nadyah's shoulders as she sashayed towards her desk.

"I will, Mistress."

Nadyah made sure there were no crumbs on her lap before she stood and curtseyed. Jael was already busy looking through her correspondence.

When the Spider gave her a nod she left the office as silently as she could.

The time at the palace would be a good distraction for her. It would be a breath of fresh air and allow her the rare opportunity to gain some distance from this life—and Varan.

PRINCESS OF DRAGA: CHAPTER TWO

ADELINA

House of Kismet
Stella di Draga
Planet Draga Terra

The hov-carriage pulled up to the House of Kismet and Princess Adelina looked through the clear plas-glass at the House that rivaled the palace in both size and opulence.

It was perched upon a cliff above the ocean with spires and towers rising high above the city. Both structures held centuries of history and resided on the shores of their shining ocean, but the House seemed dark, mysterious, and yet welcoming in a contradiction to the senses.

Adelina had managed to cajole her father into agreeing to one visit to the House of Kismet before her courtesan would move to the palace and finish her training in the bedroom arts – the *camerraleto*.

Traditionally a royal was taught in the House, but after the bombing six months ago the king had restricted all of his children to the palace unless absolutely necessary.

At first it had frustrated Adelina, as the command went against tradition and limited her already nonexistent freedom, but one visit was better than none.

A royal always began their training when they came of age to increase their value, whether it was in service to the Crown, or to their would-be spouse. The training did not come cheaply and few could afford the time and gold to obtain it.

Alpha appeared before the hov-carriage door and opened it for her. "Princess," her royal guard and best friend said quietly. His arm rose to escort her down the steps of the elegant hov-carriage.

She placed her hand over his fist and stepped down. Alpha stayed slightly behind and on her left, deferring to her higher rank despite his more dominant genetic makeup.

Gathering her spidersilk gown, she gracefully made her way through the courtyard to the massive, gold-lattice doors. Adelina stepped up the sweeping stairs before the great House of Kismet.

The afternoon sun shone warmly on her skin and the ocean breeze kept it from being oppressive. The exquisite architecture seemed to loom over her now that she stood in its shadow.

The moment overwhelmed her. Adelina felt as though she'd been waiting all her life for this. Despite the nights spent wondering and waiting for her *camerraleto* – she hesitated and one fist clutched the thin fabric of her gown tight enough to wrinkle.

Alpha gave her a sidelong glance. He knew her better than most except perhaps her sister, Giselle. He should, considering they grew up in the palace together and she'd gifted him her virginity only six months before.

They were strong companions even if they were no longer lovers.

"Are you nervous?" he whispered in case there were listening ears. And there always were.

Adelina nodded slightly. "I'm terrified," she admitted. "What if I disappoint the courtesan assigned to me? What if whoever Mistress Jael assigned isn't compatible?"

What if I can't do this?

Adelina kept the last concern to herself. She may have forgiven Alpha for putting their difference in rank between them, but it had not been an easy road. Now he stood here with her, knowing what was about to happen.

There was no one more supportive despite the strain this training put on their friendship.

"You have nothing to worry about, Princess," he reassured. Alpha's voice was firm and sure, speaking from experience it seemed.

She gave him a sly look. "Have you visited the House of Kismet as a patron?" she asked.

His infinitesimal reaction was enough. She smiled

but there was a pang of sadness that they couldn't have made things work between them. It was mixed up with the happiness that they'd been able to remain friends despite everything.

Adelina pushed thoughts of the past aside and focused on what was before her. Her coming-of-age party was less than two weeks away and she couldn't be more excited. Between that and her *camerraleto* there was much to look forward to.

As Adelina stared at the House the huge double doors opened and a gorgeous, exotic female came out – arms wide in greeting. Mistress Jael herself had come to greet her.

The last time Adelina had seen the female, it had been right after the bombings and Jael looked no different than she had on that sad day. She was utterly radiant and captivating.

Gathering her courage, Adelina stepped forward and Alpha followed as her escort. She dropped his hand when she stood only a short distance from the magnificent female.

Adelina respectfully and delicately placed her hands on Mistress Jael's arms and leaned forward, brushing her lips across the mistress's in the traditional kiss of greeting.

She released Jael and then clasped her hands in front of her out of habit and looked down at a spot on the female's chest rather than meet her dominant gaze.

This fluidity in dominance didn't matter when it came to Adelina. The scent of cactus blossom grew stronger as the mistress smiled.

Adelina had been born a true submissive. There wasn't a royal Draga who'd been born as submissive for as far back as the records went – back to the time of the Ancient Humans.

Before scientists had made genetic alterations to the human genes for survival there had been no such thing as dominance and submission in the same way she knew it to be. Adelina couldn't imagine not knowing her place in society, or where she stood with those around her.

How one was born was reflected in their personal and natural scent. It broadcasted their abilities to everyone around them and created a safe environment where those who were dominant protected those who served. She always knew who to defer to and how to act thanks to protocol.

Born with royal blood she should have been more dominant. The royal genes were programed centuries before to always remain the most dominant so as to protect their people, though the level and intensity of the dominance could vary.

Never before had a Draga royal smelled of jasmine – the sweetest scent of them all.

"Your guard may find refreshments in the carriage house with the servants." Mistress Jael indicated exactly where with a graceful flourish of her hand.

"Please follow me, Princess." Without waiting to see if Adelina would obey, Jael turned and disappeared back into the dark and mysterious House.

If they weren't on House property the break in protocol would have earned the mistress a lashing from the queen. Adelina outranked her despite their difference in dominance.

The House though, erased all rules of rank and it was a place where only gold and courtesans ruled.

Glancing over her shoulder she gave Alpha one last look. His smile was a bit strained but he shooed her after the mistress with good humor.

Adelina stepped up and into the cool hall. Mistress Jael sashayed in front of her and the dark spidersilk folds glittered in the candlelight.

She was shocked at such a crude form of light when sol-power was free and plentiful. As the flame danced and waved it cast shadows on the wall and the paintings seemed to come alive in the flickers, tricking the mind into believing. She had to admit the overall effect was rather romantic and oddly soothing.

As they walked through the opulent House, Adelina took everything in with an eager eye. The carpets were plush and an indulgent blood-red to ignite the passions. The walls were covered in black velvet scrollwork when they weren't painted with erotic scenes that made Adelina's skin tingle with the ideas suggested by the artist.

Candlelight caught the gold in Jael's gown, refocusing her attention. Everything about the female screamed sex and her mere presence put flutters in Adelina's belly. She tried not to stare at the tantalizing curves perfectly accented by a gown tailored precisely to the mistress's form.

They went through a large receiving room and

continued through a spacious public hall towards a blinding wall of light. The silk curtains were pulled aside, framing the view of the ocean. Jael opened the terrace door for her and smiled as the princess passed.

Adelina couldn't help the blush on her face.

"You will love the courtesan I have chosen for you, Princess," Jael said from behind her. There was a hint of laughter in her voice as she followed Adelina onto the expansive stone courtyard.

The warm Kala sun shone down brightly. Adelina paused and closed her eyes.

She tilted her head back and enjoyed how the sun felt on her skin. The salty tang of the ocean reached her nose and cleared the heady scent of cactus blossoms. Adelina breathed deeply and then opened her eyes, ready for the ceremony.

The terrace was on the very edge of the property and a marble courtyard reached all the way to the cliff hanging over the ocean far below them and then went out over nothing but air. Water went on endlessly to the east until it disappeared into the horizon.

Adelina glanced north and the spires of the palace jutted into the sky with the floating ramparts hovering close, surrounded by the city streets of the capitol. The massive obsidian mountains behind the palace were a stark contrast. Bright green shone on the peaks from the rain the night before.

Taking in everything, she stepped forward slowly. Columns and stacked stones created a type of open window before her that allowed one to see the glistening water beyond the statues of the gods and goddesses. Trees and plants grew everywhere.

Adelina could see a pathway on either side, each leading to gardens with differing greenery. The paths most likely led to private alcoves. Adelina blushed again as she thought of what they could be used for.

Marble pillars edged the cliff and there was a small roof over the statues of the gods and goddesses. An outside temple she realized.

Amora, the goddess of love and wisdom, was in the center where the Three-faced Goddess would normally be. Adelina wasn't surprised considering Amora was the patron goddess of the courtesans.

The goddess Amora faced inward with her back to the sea, but the spaces between each column created windows to the never-ending water. The bright sunlight glinted off the threads of gold in the marble and it sparkled.

She thought it was the most beautiful temple she had ever laid eyes on. It was simple yet exquisite.

Adelina looked to Jael who nodded. She took another step forward and dropped to her knees before the Three-faced Goddess first. She bowed low until her forehead touched the cold marble; the sun had yet to warm the statues in the temple.

"*Mia vitae se tya*," she whispered. *My life is yours.*

Then Adelina added a small plea. "Please give me the strength to find my path and help me through this experience. I do not want to disappoint my courtesan."

Slowly she rose to her feet and turned to Amora. She

knelt in front of her and bowed low, the folds of her spidersilk gown against the marble did nothing for her aching knees – though she did not bow as low as she had for the Three-faced Goddess.

The goddess of the heart had a lower rank than the Mother goddess.

Adelina then rose and sat back on her heels. Her fingers touched her heart for love and then her forehead for wisdom and finally her lips. "Grant me wisdom; to know my heart; to help me speak the truth," Adelina whispered.

She stood and brushed her spotless dress to ease her nerves before turning back to Jael.

The mistress watched her intently, no hint of sexual desire or wicked fun on her face. There was only curiosity and intelligence. When Adelina reached the Mistress of the House, her nerves grew worse in the silence.

Finally, the Jael said, "*Amarae libertov.*" *Love freely*.

The ceremony was complete.

The doors back into the House opened from the inside and the female who walked through those doors was taller than Adelina.

She had the most gorgeous sapphire eyes. They were deep, dark, and mysterious. Her hair was the color of the sun and her skin was like milk. Adelina's breath caught and she couldn't find the words to speak.

The female blushed prettily and smiled as she looked down. "Princess, I am Nadyah, your courtesan." Her voice was musical. It was lovely, warm, and throaty.

She curtseyed deeply.

It took Adelina by surprise that the courtesan would act as her submissive.

Never had Adelina met anyone less dominant than herself, and for a courtesan to believe that submission was what she needed?

Adelina was confused, but kept the frown from her face. Mentally she shook herself and brought her shoulders back ever so slightly to regain control.

"Please rise," she murmured, her heart beating faster as she realized this female was to be her instructor. "It is a pleasure to meet you, Nadyah." Adelina curtseyed back, but it was only a slight dip.

The courtesan's beauty intimidated her. Nadyah couldn't be more than a few cycles older, but she was so much more experienced. It made Adelina's heart flutter and her breath quicken to think about what she might teach her.

She blushed when she realized Jael watched her reaction with a keen eye.

Her sisters had been surprisingly close-lipped about their experiences and as Nadyah approached her with blatant desire in her eyes, Adelina could see why. The relationship between courtesan and pupil was sacred and intense.

Nadyah held out an arm for the princess and Adelina placed her hand over it in surprise. She had not expected Nadyah to escort her as a male would either.

"Would you walk with me through the gardens? I would like for us to get to know each other better."

Nadyah's voice was soft, like velvet. Adelina could lose herself in the courtesan's words.

When Adelina nodded, Nadyah looked to Jael. The mistress smiled and gave a graceful wave towards the garden path. "I hope you enjoy yourselves."

Adelina tried to ignore the way Jael watched her and the teasing in her words.

As they stepped onto the path, Nadyah led them through a copse of rare trees with blossoming fruit and the courtesan placed a hand over Adelina's. "Relax, Princess," Nadyah said softly.

Adelina followed her through the beautiful gardens, but she didn't know what to do with herself. Her nervousness had every bit of training she'd ever received deserting her.

"Tell me," Nadyah began. "How has your experience been so far?"

The question was to the point and Adelina felt her stomach tighten.

How much could the courtesan possibly know about her experience or lack thereof? Was her past on display more than she knew?

The royal family kept a livestream for the people that gave them all glimpses into their life and allowed the people to see how they handled the kingdom as every decision made a difference in every citizen's life. They were then edited into a pleasing stream.

But the recorders were only allowed into certain areas of their private lives.

"Your guard is a very handsome one," she said simply.

Somehow Nadyah knew.

Adelina wasn't sure if she was angry about it or not, but this female was to be her companion for the next few months. It was in her best interest to confide in her. "Yes he is," she whispered. "Briefly we were involved."

Nadyah didn't react to the confession in any way that could have embarrassed her which Adelina was intensely grateful for. The courtesan patted her hand gently. "Please tell me about this experience?"

The weight of sadness settled over Adelina like a cloak and she shouldered it with familiarity. "Six months ago, I was finally able to confess my feelings to him after cycles of pining." She hated the word but it was true.

With a sigh Adelina trailed her fingertips over the black roses her father had gifted to the House – the sacred *rosanera*. The rose garden perfumed the warm summer air and she breathed it in.

"After the tour of the system was cut short I kissed him." Adelina couldn't bring herself to look at Nadyah yet.

The garden path took them out to the edge of the cliff and the view was spectacular. A bench was in the perfect position to watch the waves down below, to enjoy the ocean, and the feel of the sun.

Adelina sat delicately on the hard stone bench and Nadyah lounged next to her. One arm went over the back and she propped her head on her hand, turning her body to face Adelina.

She had the courtesan's undivided attention and it unnerved her.

Adelina picked at the folds of her skirt, keeping her head down. It was still difficult for her to talk about. "He was my first and only," she finally managed. "I loved him and he loved me. The night after I gave him my virginity we discovered the Neprijat had attacked our Corinthian allies in the Khara System." Adelina shuddered as she remembered the vid and waved her hand indicating Nadyah knew the rest of the events that day.

The Neprijat had ravaged the Khara royal family in unspeakable ways. Then later that very same day the Draga royal announcement of King Orion's retirement, and Raena's coronation fifty cycles earlier than expected were made.

The Announcement's Balcony had been bombed during the event. Adelina was unaware if Nadyah knew she had almost died that day.

It had been too close.

Alpha had been so shaken at the close call he had blamed himself – and her.

"He ended the relationship because he was distracted by me. Alpha felt as though he might have noticed something earlier, seen something not quite right before the bombs went off. He said he should have gotten to me sooner at the very least as my personal guard." Adelina shrugged.

Alpha had saved her life.

"It didn't matter to him that we loved each other. The possibility of a promotion to prince never even occurred to him." Then she finally looked up at Nadyah. "Because of that I let him go."

As her father had said, she needed someone she didn't have to convince to marry her.

There were tears in Nadyah's eyes and she cupped Adelina's cheek gently. "I apologize, Princess. I'm a terrible romantic and your story makes my heart ache."

When it happened, Adelina had only cried the once. Her eyes had been dry ever since, but seeing Nadyah's tears caused a knot to form in her throat.

She hated crying. It was shameful, and more emotion than she was ever allowed to express publicly.

Nadyah gave her a quick little hug before sitting back to look at her. "Would the king have allowed the marriage?" she asked, wiping the wetness from her cheeks.

Adelina nodded. "Even if Alpha hadn't grown up in the palace with me, even if my father hadn't taken him on as his ward after Alpha's parents died – the king would have allowed me to marry a guard. Who I married didn't matter to him then, as long as I was happy."

The sound of the crashing waves soothed her heart and Adelina took a deep breath of the salty ocean air to clear her head.

Nadyah missed nothing. "At the time," she murmured. "But now?"

"Now he is dying," Adelina whispered.

Still hardly able to admit it to herself, she couldn't deny the clear evidence of what her eyes saw. Every day it looked as though the king wasted away a bit more and soon there would be nothing left of him.

"Raena will be queen in a matter of weeks and she

has no children of her own. That makes the rest of us her heirs."

The courtesan composed herself and her expression became thoughtful as she tapped the bench with one lacquered nail. Adelina wondered how she got them to stay so dark and blue.

"Because you will become the second in line to the throne, your options will need to be open and the possibility of matches for the benefit of the kingdom will be required."

Adelina nodded. "Raena promised I would be able to choose, but what will be allowed might be limited."

She shook her head, the annoyance raged to the surface before she could squash it. "Our father always allowed us the opportunity to find love and I never wanted to marry for political gain. My dream was to find real and lasting love, someone who I could spend the next two or three hundred cycles with if the Three-faced Goddess was generous."

She breathed deep and tried to remind herself her parents had an arranged marriage and now they were deeply in love.

Love freely.

Anything was possible.

Nadyah said nothing. She didn't even move. Those deep sapphire eyes simply watched her – studying, assessing, and measuring. "So you gave your guard your virginity, but it didn't work out romantically which means you've only had intercourse the one time. You are still friends, yes?"

Adelina remembered this was Nadyah's profession. She was supposed to know these things in detail. She nodded in confirmation. "I have no experience other than Alpha."

It was strange to think about it so clinically. It never occurred to her to play like her sisters and brothers did. She'd loved Alpha for so many cycles she never had eyes for anyone else.

The last six months had been an ongoing nightmare and she had very little time to consider any other lovers.

At least in that time she had been able to repair her friendship with her guard. She would have been truly heartbroken if she'd lost her best friend.

Nadyah's soothing cactus blossom sent washed over her as the courtesan stood and offered her hand to Adelina. "Come with me," she said. "You need to relax and get comfortable so we can continue our conversation." Her gentle smile eased some of Adelina's stress.

She placed her hand in the courtesan's and let her lead them back to the House.

PRINCESS OF DRAGA: CHAPTER THREE

ADELINA

House of Kismet
Stella di Draga
Planet Draga Terra

Nadyah navigated the shadowy halls deftly.

They passed a dining room with guests who came to enjoy the meals. There was an entertainment room, a ladies' solar, and a gentlemen's parlor. Adelina caught sight of the library and nearly pulled her courtesan to a stop, but she was too curious to spend the little time she had in the House with books she was sure they had at the palace.

Perhaps Nadyah could bring a few to the palace that they might not have, and she could always come back. Adelina knew if her father didn't consent there were ways around the orders.

Her thoughts had distracted her long enough to get

her to Nadyah's room without fainting. But the second the door closed behind them her heart pounded hard enough to make breathing difficult.

Adelina clasped her hands in front of her to hide the trembling in her hands, but Nadyah was too well trained and she saw everything.

"Relax," the courtesan murmured. "You have nothing to fear here, or from me. You are the one in control. I am under your command." Nadyah sank to her knees before Adelina in demonstration – submissive and demure.

For the first time in her life someone knelt before her.

Adelina felt a spark of desire burn away some of her anxiety. The reaction shocked her. Adelina was a true submissive. Being in a dominant position should have made her uncomfortable. It usually did, enough to give her a panic attack. But in the safety of Nadyah's room she had no one else to compete with.

Adelina gently touched her golden hair and Nadyah looked up with a small smile. "May I stand?" she asked.

The spark turned into a flame at her words. Silently Adelina nodded, shocked at her own reaction.

Nadyah stood and kept her eyes down. The courtesan smiled softly as she walked around Adelina. Gently her delicate fingers brushed the back of Adelina's neck and the princess shivered.

A molten fire began to rage within her and the anticipation made her tremble. Finally, Adelina would learn the secrets of the *camerraleto*, and this beautiful female would show her.

The thought struck her like lightning and her body

responded. The fire in her stomach spread to between her legs as Nadyah's fingers trailed along her shoulders and down her back. She gasped in surprise. Adelina wanted Nadyah to touch her and the realization left her slick.

Then the courtesan led her to the massive bed in the adjoining room. "Lie face down," she murmured.

Adelina did as she asked, resting her head on her pillowed arms.

Nadyah slowly, seductively undid each button down her back and then pulled her dress down – down until she heard the spidersilk pool on the floor. Goose-pimples ran over her skin in anticipation and she clenched her legs as the fire seemed to grow.

"May I help you relax, Princess?" Nadyah asked. Her sweet, sultry voice was right next to Adelina's ear. Her breath tickled and Adelina couldn't help her tiny gasp.

It was all she could do to nod in acceptance, wondering what a courtesan considered relaxed.

There was a tiny clink of glass and the scent of peppermint reached Adelina's nose. Nadyah's soft, warm hands stroked her back and shoulders, working the tight muscles. Adelina sighed and closed her eyes in bliss. This was not what she had expected but it was exactly what she needed.

The tight muscles started to loosen under the expert touch while Nadyah massaged her shoulders and back.

Adelina sighed as she memorized everything she'd seen.

Nadyah's hands on her back made her almost sleepy.

She couldn't remember the last time she had felt so relaxed.

"Were you born to this House?" Adelina asked.

Nadyah's words seemed to caress her skin as she spoke. "I was born in this city, Stella di Draga – the shining star of our planet," she said. "Stella di Draga has been my home my entire life. But I didn't join the House until I was a few cycles old."

The courtesan was silent for a moment. "Do you have any expectations for our time together? Any specific skills you had in mind to acquire?"

Adelina shook her head. "I have none, only the need to know what can help me gather the information I might need to serve the Crown, and maybe for a future spouse."

Nadyah's hands stilled at her words and Adelina's eyes flew open as she wondered what she had said to cause such a reaction.

She tensed as she waited for a response. She was a royal courtesan, which meant she had to know what was expected of Adelina, right?

"You mean to seduce someone for information?" Nadyah clarified.

Adelina glanced over her shoulder at the courtesan and studied her for a moment but the female kept her eyes down and resumed her work. Adelina lay her head back on her arms and decided it wouldn't hurt to answer. Every courtesan was required to sign a contract with a promise to keep royal secrets to themselves.

"If I need to, yes. I hope to travel as an ambassador and report back what I can."

The smell of peppermint cleansed the air of the strong cactus blossom scent. "I can teach you everything you need to know and more."

Nadyah moved slightly, kneading Adelina's shoulders as she leaned forward and Adelina felt her courtesan's breasts press into her bare skin – intentional or not, she wasn't sure.

Those silky hands stroked downwards and this time they didn't stop when they reached the small of her back. Her hands trailed over Adelina's ass and down the inside of her thighs to innocently massage the back of her legs.

Desire rippled through Adelina like wildfire.

There was an ache deep inside and her clit pulsed. She shuddered, partially in pleasure and partially in embarrassment. It had been months and she'd nearly forgotten how intense her reaction to desire could be.

Nadyah massaged her thighs, getting closer and closer to where Adelina needed her to be. She tried not to clench her them together as it would be a tell-tale sign.

"You are beautiful, Princess. You are powerful and anyone would be lucky to have your attentions," Nadyah said as she worked Adelina's tense muscles.

A feather-touch of Nadyah's finger over her slick folds was so brief Adelina wondered if she had imagined it, but her skin burned in response and she nearly couldn't resist her own wanton desire.

Nadyah moved on to her calves and the innocent touches were almost unbearable. She wanted Nadyah to take her.

It made her want to flip over and give herself to the female's expertise.

"I may outrank anyone but my family," Adelina managed to say, breathing slowly to try and control her reaction. "But I am not a powerful person. I am the most submissive there is."

Nadyah was silent for a moment. "Sometimes the submissives are the ones with the most power. They draw strong dominants to them and incite the age-old instinct to protect and defend. You do not have to be the strongest or the most dominant to wield those who are. Have you ever done something you haven't wanted to do without good reason?"

Her words jolted Adelina out of her sudden need, enough to clear her head. "No, I haven't," she admitted slowly.

Could submissives really hold their own, more subtle power?

"Not all strength looks the same." Nadyah then started a foot massage.

Her quiet work allowed Adelina to seriously reconsider her life. It was so simple, how could she have overlooked something so obvious?

"We can start with subtle seduction," Nadyah said.

Her timing was so perfect it was eerie. She always knew exactly when to stay silent and when to speak.

"Body language is the most important part of this seduction," the courtesan murmured. "The rest is simple enough. How to dress, how to make yourself up to incite the response you are looking for is all a part of the subtlety. There is always the dance of dominance and rank. As you will outrank everyone this will be simple enough, but the dance among other royals is a bit more dangerous. They will all identify your lack of dominance through your scent."

Nadyah slid off the bed, slinky and graceful. Her fingertips trailed up Adelina's leg, over the curve of her ass, and up her back. "I've never smelled jasmine so sweet." Her courtesan brushed her lips over Adelina's forehead.

Adelina shivered. This female had her acting like a lovesick male.

With genuine care the courtesan brushed the princess's hair back from her face. "I assume you understand from your training as princess how to properly interact with those who are more dominant than you are, and how to properly hold your position."

She nodded. It was no easy thing to uphold her rank over someone she wanted to submit to. Adelina had worked hard to keep her shy nature from hindering the work she needed to do.

Nadyah held out a hand and Adelina took it, trusting the courtesan completely. She led Adelina to stand before her. "As females we may be naturally, physically weaker than males, but we have silent strengths and one of them is the ability to control males."

She gave Adelina a quick look. "Even if you prefer females you will need to deal with the males at court and as an ambassador."

Adelina stood naked before the courtesan and

refrained from crossing her arms over her breasts. Her nipples hardened under Nadyah's scrutiny and she reminded herself to pay attention.

"My lovely," Nadyah murmured as her eyes trailed from Adelina's head to her toes and back again. "You are exquisite."

She pulled Adelina's shoulders back. "Not only does this make you appear more confident, it pushes your breasts out. Despite how irritating it is that males are so distracted by them, use it to your advantage. It sometimes pays for them to be addle-minded."

Adelina nodded in response to the courtesan's words. These were all things she'd been taught before, but never for these reasons. Nadyah trailed her fingers along the princess's collarbone and pressed her lips to the hollow between Adelina's neck and shoulder before pulling back to search her purple eyes.

"You are a princess. You know what you want and what you do not."

Nadyah turned her to face the large mirror in her closet. Adelina knew this would be the most important part of her *camerraleto*.

Adelina was shy and nervous with anxiety that sometimes crippled. She needed to come into her own – not shedding a skin exactly, but building a second one.

"Being shy is one thing, but feeling self-conscious is something else entirely," Nadyah said. "If you feel shy, use it to your advantage. Keep your voice low enough they have to lean in to hear you, as if you were telling them a secret," she explained with a wicked grin.

Adelina's eyes widened as the courtesan drew closer, her voice lowering in example. "Touch lightly, but briefly." Her fingers skimmed the inside of Adelina's wrist for a brief moment before she withdrew.

The courtesan circled Adelina and tipped up her chin. "The key is eye contact when you can manage it. Eye contact alone will make you seem more confident. Be comfortable with who you are and make no apology for your feelings."

Then Nadyah stopped in front of Adelina, blocking the mirror so she had to look at her. Gently Nadyah kissed her cheek.

Adelina took in her words and made them her own, wrapping them around her like silk.

"I am going to pick something for you to wear. Your gowns are beautiful, but they are sweet and demure. We want to remind everyone you will be of age."

Nadyah tucked a golden strand of hair behind her ear and went into her closet. She rifled through what seemed like endless dresses and finally chose something. It was a magnificent gold spidersilk dress that would enhance Adelina's golden tan and blacker-than-night hair.

"Put that on. I have something that will pair beautifully with it." Nadyah started looking through her drawers and Adelina turned to the mirror.

The dress slid over her legs like water as she pulled it up over her hips. The material clung to her waist and Adelina slipped her arms through the sleeves. The wider straps gave more support so that the plunging V-neck draped just right over her breasts. The V ended just above her navel and Adelina felt nerves gather.

Never had she worn something so daring, so sexual.

Yet, the spidersilk was the perfect gold and the skirts draped and billowed in all the right places. There was a subtle slit that went all the way up to her thigh, but only a small flash of skin would show as she walked unless she crossed her legs.

It suited her despite everything.

Adelina pulled her shoulders back and there was a slight curve of her breast showing. Amora save her, Nadyah knew exactly what she was doing.

The courtesan gave her a knowing smile as she came out of her closet with something glittering in her palm. "That dress has never suited me. I am almost positive that client is colorblind. I am too fair for such a thing, but on you? Darling, your guard will be wishing he'd never said such foolish things to break your heart."

She smiled back at Nadyah and felt better about the amount of skin showing for all the world to see. The slippers she wore wouldn't suit, but this was a dress she would want to wear with heels to add height to her small frame.

For the first time in her life she wished she had larger breasts to fill out such a dress, but the Goddess knew she didn't really want them. Raena never stopped complaining about the back pain.

"I want you to have this," Nadyah said, holding out a glittering strand of gold with a fat gem hanging from it. "Think of it as my coming-of-age present to you."

Adelina's eyes widened when she saw the octagonal amethyst precisely the color of her eyes. "I can't possibly accept such a gift," she stammered.

The piece was perfect and worth more than Nadyah could know. Adelina would never take advantage of her; she of all people knew exactly what gems were worth.

"I have jewels and gems enough to rival even you and your family. My patrons are generous." Nadyah's smile was wicked and she placed the necklace on Adelina, clasping it before she could protest further.

Adelina watched in the mirror as the gold chain formed a choker around her neck and a single strand fell from the hollow of her throat, leaving the amethyst nestled between her breasts.

It accented the gown and her coloring perfectly.

Her mouth dropped open in shock and her hand went to the glittering rock. The rope chain had to have three or four strands twisted to hold the five karat amethyst, but the work was so well done she couldn't see the separate strands with her naked eye.

Nadyah looked unsure for the first time since she had met her. "You probably already have plans for the upcoming events but perhaps we can recreate your wardrobe in time. We will begin practicing immediately and I want to help you go through your clothes and jewels to properly showcase your assets. For the most part we will keep the changes subtle. You can wear this on a romantic evening or even for the noble's reception."

The courtesan tapped her lower lip with one of her lacquered nails. "What do you think?"

Adelina always prided herself on her work and was unsure this change would be for the best. "I design most of my own wardrobe," she admitted.

She was hesitant to tell Nadyah. No one but her siblings really knew about her hobbies. She liked to keep them off the livestream when she could.

Nadyah's face lit up. "This is wonderful! Let's see what we can do to open you up a bit more." Her wink eased some of Adelina's fears and she felt closer to Nadyah than she thought she would on their first meeting.

"I will show you my work when you arrive at the palace tomorrow," Adelina told her. "Father has given you a room adjoining mine. It was originally meant for my spouse, but we both agreed this made sense."

Adelina was nervous about the accommodations. Never had a courtesan lived at the palace aside from Elara.

As she removed the dress, Adelina checked the time-keeper on the nightstand. Their time at the House was almost up. She had one last question to ask Nadyah that she hadn't had the courage to ask until now.

She slipped on her own gown and watched as Nadyah packed the dress and a few others into a beautiful box.

"May I ask you something?"

Instantly Nadyah focused on her. "You may ask me anything, Princess."

Adelina pulled at her dress until it fell as it should

and then picked at her fingernails. How would she explain?

"The few times Alpha and I were...intimate I had a curious reaction," she managed. Adelina could feel the heat on her cheeks and hated it in that moment.

She threw up her hands in exasperation at herself. "I lost all control. I could not stop myself from reacting in a way no virgin would have. My skin itched terribly and I wanted him more than I wanted anything else. At the time I did not care if we were in public or not. I have never heard of something like this, but I thought there might be a chance you would know."

A courtesan would know more about desire and physical reactions than anyone else in Draga.

Nadyah frowned and Adelina's heart sank. What would she do if her courtesan did not have an answer for her?

"Did this same feeling occur earlier during the massage?"

Adelina couldn't hold her gaze. Her eyes dropped to the floor and she blushed furiously. This was a clinical question though and not a conquest. "Yes."

The intense speculation on Nadyah's face worried her. She studied Adelina so closely for a brief second it left her breathless.

"No control whatsoever?"

At Adelina's nod she made a small noise as she contemplated. "I will look into this. It is unusual, but there should be an answer in the library. If not, Mistress Jael will know where I can find what I need."

"Thank you, Nadyah." Adelina whispered, and she truly meant it.

Perhaps there was something wrong with her genetics. After all, she was a submissive royal which shouldn't be possible. Her genes were bred into her, designed centuries ago by the Ancients – the humans of old.

It was part of their animalistic nature brought back in force, designed to create a wolf-like society. She had always wondered how terrible things must have gotten for the Ancient Humans to create such a design.

Then she always wondered how she could possibly have genes that would set her so far apart from her family. Adelina wasn't even on the Draga royal spectrum of dominance.

"Let us get you dressed and then we will have a small meal before our departure." Nadyah was smiling again, but her sexual intensity was subdued.

Adelina only hoped the trust she'd bestowed on the courtesan hadn't been a terrible mistake.

∽

Get the full book here:
Princess of Draga.

OTHER BOOKS

EMMA DEAN

THE DRAGA COURT SERIES

Princess of Draga

Crown of Draga

Jasmine of Draga

Heir of Draga

Queen of Draga

Warrior Prince of Hai

Fate of Draga

Prequel Novella – Royal Guard of Draga*

Christmas Epilogue Novella - Winter Solstice in Draga

*Can be read as a standalone before or after Princess of Draga, but in the timeline takes place before Princess.

Want updates on when the books are released and my

progress with them?

Sign up for my newsletter @ emmadeanromance.com

DOMINANCE

Each Kalan is born with a scent marker that identifies their level of dominance. There is also a spectrum within each level. Two people who are at the same level, such as the black rose - *rosanera*, can have a different amount of dominance.

The spicier or muskier the scent, the more dominant. The sweeter, the more submissive.

The genetic alterations used these scent markers to reflect ability and position in a pack or society like the Ancient wolves.

From most dominant to least:
Black Rose/*Rosanera*
Winter-flowers
Orange Blossom
Lilac
Jasmine

HOUSES OF DRAGA

IN ORDER FROM CLOSEST TO FARTHEST FROM THE KALA SUN

Deytis – Barony
　Baron Kace and Baroness Lyria
　Heir – Leo
　Second-born – Lora

Draga – Royals
　King Orion and Queen Adele
　Heir – Raena
　Second-born – Giselle
　Third-born – Adelina
　Fourth-born – Asher
　Fifth-born – William
　Sixth in line to the throne – Ian, Mistress Elara's son
　Brother to the King – Prince Solomon
　His wife, Princess Mara
　First-born – Ajax
　Second-born – Vasara

HOUSES OF DRAGA

Avvis – Archduchy
Archduchess Indra and Archduke Chet
Heir – Hayden
Second-born – Masha
Indra's Sister – Lady Tine
Her husband Lord Berter
First-born – Sonya
Second-born – Hewayn
Indra's brother – Lord Keve

Priea – Marquis
Marquess Delia and Marquis Greyson
Heir – Veri
Second-born – Alock
Third-born – Cindra
Cousins – Adam
Alfonso

Ushanov – Duchy
Duchess Odette and Duke Mikel
Heir – Marcel
Second-born – Rashad
Third-born – Raphael

Pedranus – Count-ship
Countess Joslynn

Scyria – Count-ship
Countess Malaya

Heir – Anatoly
His wife – Elena
Second-born – Peter
Third-born – Sirus

Treon – Marquis
Marquis Peter and Marquess Wendy
Heir – Lucas
Second-born – Grady

Seprilles – Barony
Baron Jarvis, Baron Romeo, and Baroness Leslie
Heir – Jayden
Second-born – Rory

THE DRAGA SYSTEM

PLANETS IN THE DRAGA SYSTEM FROM FIRST TO LAST

The race of Humans living in the Draga system under the Kala sun is called Kalans. Only the ruling family of each planet holds the name Draga, Avvis, etc.

Sun – Kala
    Deytis – Barony
    Draga Terra – Capitol; Royal Planet
    Avvis – Archduchy
    Priea – Marquis
    Ushanov – Duchy
    Pedranus – Count-ship
    Scyria – Count-ship
    Treon** – Marquis
    Seprilles** – Barony

**Seprilles and Treon have elliptical orbits around the sun. Half of the cycle one planet is on the border of one

THE DRAGA SYSTEM

side of the galaxy, and the other half is on the opposite border. Twice a year they are closest to each other than any other planet.

THE KHARA SYSTEM

PLANETS IN THE KHARA SYSTEM FROM FIRST TO LAST

The race of Humans living in the Khara system under the Corinth sun is called the Corinthians.

Sun – Corinth

Capuli – Panthera House
Prince Milagros and Princess Lilja alive

Arcadius – Neofilis House
Princess Kaita alive

Khara Prime – Capitol
(Where the current ruling family resides)
Royals Dead

Minara – Tigris House
Prince Valdis alive

Lithios – Jaguar House
　　Princess Svana and Princess Tawney alive

Leva – Leo House
　　Royals Dead. Prince Nash's home planet

Kepri – Serval House
　　Royals Dead

THE HAI SYSTEM

PLANETS IN THE HAI SYSTEM FROM FIRST TO LAST

The race of Humans living in the Hai galaxy under the Drakesthai sun is called the Drakesthai. This does not apply to the Humans who remain Unchanged.

Sun – Drakesthai

Anarr – Skye Dragons
- Zoya
- Eduard
- Kaiden
- Roman
- Leo
- Alexei
- Mikhail
- Viktor

Kuan-Yin – Ruled by the Unchanged

Imaldi – Ruled by the Unchanged

Hai Delta – Capitol; Obsidian Dragons
Serilda
Rykian
Jaxon
Kalene

Tainos – Fyre Dragons
Vasili

Argo – Starr Dragons
Aleksandr
Dimitri

Vudu Shaa – Vega Dragons
Tatsuo

ABOUT THE AUTHOR

Emma Dean is the author of Draga Court and the Council of Paranormals. Juggling work, life, higher education, and a rambunctious toddler leaves little room for much else, but when she gets the chance she dives into a good book and likes to re-read the Black Jewels series by Anne Bishop every year during Christmas.

Follow her on Social Media or
www.emmadeanromance.com

facebook.com/emmadeanromance
bookbub.com/authors/emma-dean
amazon.com/Emma-Dean/e/B073Z3XZ4X

Made in the USA
Columbia, SC
21 December 2024